CONFESSIO

Timothy Lea

Running a sea-side hotel with brother-in-law Sidney seems right up Timmy's street. But the trouble is that soon it's a question of when to stop running. The staff are sex-mad—or just plain mad—and the lady visitors!

Some need assistance on their wedding night, others a release from the boredom of being rugby widows. And, of course, there is always the notorious Pendulum Society—husband-swappers to a woman—to keep Timmy at full stretch. Can he keep it up?

What a question to ask the hardened survivor of

Confessions of a Window Cleaner
Confessions of a Driving Instructor
Confessions from a Holiday Camp

Confessions from a Hotel

TIMOTHY LEA

SPHERE BOOKS LIMITED
London and Sydney

First published in Great Britain by Sphere Books Ltd 1973
30–32 Gray's Inn Road, London WC1X 8JL
Copyright © Christopher Wood 1973
Reprinted 1973, 1974, 1975, 1977, 1978, 1980, 1981, 1984

Publisher's Note

TRADE
MARK

Set in Intertype Times Roman

Printed and bound in Great Britain by
Collins, Glasgow

CONFESSIONS FROM A HOTEL

Chapter One

In which Timothy returns from foreign climes in the exhausting company of Nat and Nan and finds that brother-in-law, Sidney, has been invalided out of Funfrall Enterprises in unusual circumstances.

Chapter Two

In which Timmy accompanies Sidney to the Cromby, a dilapidated seaside hotel the latter has bought, and meets some of the staff. Amongst them Sandra, June and Audrey; girls who are prepared to bend over backwards to please the new owners.

Chapter Three

In which Timmy meets Miss Ruperts and Mrs. Caitley, the cook, and starts at the bottom. Also, in which he receives a surprise visit from June, Audrey and a new friend, Carmen, and in turn surprises Sidney.

Chapter Four

In which Timmy helps a newly wed couple overcome their problems with the aid of personal example and the invention of the Cromby Photographic Club, a group who specialise in not so still lives.

Chapter Five

In which a punch-up breaks out in the dining room and Timmy is able to assist Mrs. Beecham, an American lady whose husband falls victim to a practical joke on their wedding night. This assistance being interrupted by an unusual visitor.

Chapter Six

In which Sid and Timmy have a brush with an unlovable property developer called Rigby, and a wife-swapping club arrives for the weekend. Timmy spends the night with one of their lady members who has an unusual hobby.

Chapter Seven

In which mum, dad, and sister Rosie arrive for the week-end and Rosie threatens to succumb to the charms of one Sam the Ram. The family visit an entertainment on the pier which ends abruptly, and a dance at the Cromby gets out of hand and is brought to a watery close.

Chapter Eight

In which the Old Rottingfestrians rugby team arrives on tour, and Timmy entertains one of the wives who prefers in-door games. Doctor Walter Carboy, a gentleman with expensive tastes, books in at the hotel.

Chapter Nine

In which Doctor Carboy is revealed and there is a show-down with Rigby, the property developer. A member of the Old Rottingfestrians takes a long drive off a short pier and the O.R. ladies organise an entertainment for Timmy and Sid.

CHAPTER ONE

I don't know how you would handle four weeks on a tramp steamer with a couple of nymphomaniacs, but I was right knackered at the end of it, I can tell you. The second mate was carried off the boat on a stretcher, and he managed to barricade himself in his cabin after the first week. By the cringe it was a voyage and a half. Now I know what they mean when they say "see Naples and die". Nat and Nan found me skulking in an empty lifeboat the night before we docked and I nearly kicked the bucket with my first glimpse of Mount Vesuvius. Talk about insatiable—I can now, because I looked it up in the dictionary—if those two birds were rabbits it would not have needed myxomatosis to kill off half the male bunny population. I am not unpartial to a bit of the other but—blimey! There is a limit. After the first couple of hours it is becoming more a penance than a penis if you know what I mean.

Anyway, for the sake of those of you who missed my capers as a Holiday Host with Funfrall Enterprises, I had better explain what I am on about. My period of service on an island off the Costa Brava had come to an end for a number of reasons—not the least of them being that my dad had burned down the camp. Accidentally, of course. Everything dad does is an accident, which accounts for how I happen to be about to write this. Anyway, that is another story and I would be the last person to put anybody off their cornflakes by telling it.

My presence on the boat with Nat and Nan—my pen starts shaking uncontrollably every time I write their names —is occasioned by me being left to clear up after the blaze. Once I have sifted all the dentures out of the ashes and paid off the local labour, I am expected to make my way home on a battered tramp steamer calling at every port in the Mediterranean. I would not normally be the first person to start whining about such treatment, were it not for the presence of the deadly duo already alluded to. Also, another lively bird called Carmen who fortunately gets homesick after a couple of days and dives overboard to join a passing fishing boat. Nat and Nan have the same attitude towards sex as those small birds that eat ten times their own weight every day, only in their case, forget small birds and substitute bleeding great vultures. Not that they are unattractive, oh, dear me, no. They are beautiful girls and living tributes to the efficacy of National Health Milk and free dental care. The only trouble is that they do have this disconcerting habit of tearing the trousers off every bloke they meet. And on a few thousand square feet of tramp steamer it gets so it is not worth putting your trousers on again. Your turn is going to come up in another few minutes, buster, so lie back and enjoy it.

Luckily, I have had experience of these girls (I laugh hollowly as I write that) and for the first few days I manage to keep out of the way while the crew run amok. By the end of the first week they are running a mile. Every time the Terrible Twins come round a corner, the sleek smiles slide off their greasy faces faster than blobs of fat off a hot plate. By the end of the second week they are threatening mutiny and by the end of the third week they have twice tried to abandon ship in a lifeboat. One bloke dives overboard the minute we get into the Bay of Naples. How he finds the strength to reach shore, I will never know.

My attempts to avoid being pressed into service—a not altogether happy, but very accurate description of what takes place—founder on my natural desire for food. I am intercepted on a sneaky trip to the galley and from that moment on I am making progress towards a frayed tonk like every other male on board.

By the time we get to Liverpool I never want to see another woman as long as I live—or at least two weeks—and the crew have burned all their pin-ups. The captain has not been seen for four days. Every time anybody taps on the door of his cabin a feeble voice keeps repeating—"Don't let them get me. Remember the R.N.V.R." The poor basket has obviously gone round the twist.

8

When we get to Scouseland and can actually see the Liver Building the crew fall on their knees like pilgrims getting their first eyeful of Mecca. There is hardly an Englishman amongst them but they all know that this is where the girls get off. The expression of unspeakable joy on their faces as we go down the gangplank is something I will always remember.

My own feelings are typical of those of any son of Albion returning to the land of his birth—bitter disappointment. When I was on the Isla de Amor I could not wait to feel the native sod under my feet but now as I see some of the native sods in person I wish I was back in the land of the antique plumbing. At least there was sunshine there and I could not understand the newspaper headlines. My tan has been fading since the Bay of Biscay and mum and dad and Scraggs Lane seem about as tempting as two weeks in a Leper Colony.

But that is not my immediate problem. Having seen Nat and Nan closing fast with a group of unsuspecting dockers, I have legged it off in the opposite direction and made my way swiftly to Lime Street station. This being the point of departure for The Smoke, and the bosom of my family. It is mid-morning and British Rail's excellent inter-city service is decidedly under-patronised. I buy a copy of a book called 'John Adam—Samurai', which looks as if it has a few juicy moments, and settle down to a couple of hours of peace and quiet. Outside the compartment the sun is breaking through and my spirits begin to lift. Maybe dear old England is not so bad after all.

"Ah, so there you are! Creeping off without saying goodbye. That wasn't very kind to your little playmates, was it?"

"Decidedly unkind, I should say. Not the sort of behaviour Uncle Giles would like, eh Sis?"

Yes, folks; it is Nat and Nan, the girls who gave up the idea of group marriage because they could not find a group large enough. I should mention that the Uncle Giles they refer to is Sir Giles Slat, Chairman of Funfrall Enterprises, the grave concern that is employing me—and hopefully

9

paying me some much needed moola for my heroic efforts during the last few weeks.

"After all, we've been through," says Nat reproachfully.

"Speak for yourself," I snarl. "Now for God's sake leave me alone. You lay one finger on me and I'll pull the communication cord."

"It won't do any good, darling. The train isn't moving yet. I'm very disappointed in you, Timmy. I thought we had a chance of liberating you but you're still very uptight, aren't you?" That is another thing about these nutty birds. They believe that if everybody sublimated their aggressions in sexual activity there would be no more wars. That is their excuse, anyway.

"Take your hand out of my trousers," I say. "Uptight? After what I've had to endure in the last four weeks? I'm slacker than a four-inch nut on a toothpick." Nat draws away from me reproachfully and the train jerks into motion.

"I was hoping we were going to be able to put in a glowing report about you to Uncle Gilesy," she says. "But if you persist in continuing to be a reactionary slave to bourgeois convention." She shakes her head sadly.

"What do you mean?" I say nervously.

"I mean, Timmykins, we may have to tell Nunky that you were very naughty on the boat. That you forced us to cohabit with the crew."

"Forced! Those poor bastards are paddling that boat out to sea with their bare hands in order to get away from you."

"They did have problems," says Nat sadly.

"They *did* have. But they don't any longer. When are you two birds going to wise up to the fact that everybody doesn't want to get laid all the time?"

"We could say he confessed to burning down the camp," says Nan.

"Hey, wait a minute!"

"That's a good idea. Uncle Gilesy won't like that, will he?"

"Timmy will go to prison for arson. Poor Timmy."

"You do that and I'll—" I rack my brains for something I will do.

"You'll do what?" says Nan. "There's nothing you can tell Uncle Giles about us that he doesn't know already."

"On the other hand, we might suggest some form of bonus as being in order. Nunky is very hot on rewarding loyal staff."

"And I'm just very hot," says Nat beginning to pull down the blinds.

"Just for Auld Lang Syne," says Nan as she starts to undo my shirt buttons. "We may never see each other again."

"You're dead right there," I say. "Once this bleeding thing stops, you'll need running shoes to keep up with me."

"He's beautiful when he's mad, isn't he?" says Nat.

"Beautiful. Come on, give us a little kiss."

Outside the landscape is flashing past at about eighty miles an hour, otherwise I might try to throw myself through the window.

"Somebody's going to come," I gulp.

"You never know your luck."

"I mean a ticket collector or somebody."

"Well, we've all got tickets, haven't we? It just says don't lean out of the window. And we're not going to do it hanging out of the window, are we?"

"I don't know," says Nat thoughtfully. "It sounds rather fun. Supposing—"

"No!" I scream. "Oh my God. What am I going to do?"

"We know you know the answer to that one," soothes Nan. "Remember how much fun it was on the beach?"

"Yes. But there weren't millions of people wandering about there."

"The train is empty, darling."

"We could go in one of the loos," says Nan, "but I hate stand-up quickies and it would be awfully cramping."

I look at the pictures of some Scottish river on the wall and wish I could be there. The cool water closing over my head—

"So, you're going to say something good about me, are

11

you?" I say. I mean if there is going to be no escape, I might as well get the best deal I can.

"I hope so, love-bunny," murmurs Nat into my half-nibbled ear. "Now, let's see if you're going to be a good boy."

Her hand fondles the region of my thigh and finds what it is looking for. "Oh yes, I like that."

"Me too." Nan pops open the buttons of my jeans and slips her hand into the one-way system of my Y-fronts. "You shouldn't wear these," she scolds. "You should let him breathe."

"He seems to be coming up for air now," says Nat with interest, as she starts yanking down my pants.

That's the amazing thing about my John Thomas. It seems to lead an existence totally independent of the rest of me. My brain may be saying run for the hills but my J.T. never seems to hear it. Given the presence of a friendly lady it will lumber fitfully into an upright position and stand there waiting for the best to happen. At moments like this its touching eagerness to please is beyond price.

"I'm on a bonus, then, am I?"

"You should be doing this for love, not money," says Nat as she helps my jeans over my heels. "We really have failed with you, haven't we?"

"You're blackmailing me, so you can't talk."

"I don't want to talk, angel. I want you to start probing me with your lovely instrument."

"You always go first," sniffs Nat.

"No, I don't."

"Yes you do."

"Alright. We'll toss for it. Which ball have I got in my hand?"

"The left one."

"You looked."

"I didn't."

"Do you mind!" I interrupt. "I'm not a bloody bumper car, you know."

"You give a much smoother ride, don't you Timmy?—oh look!"

12

She is referring to the way my J.T. leaps into the air in sympathy when one of the blinds suddenly whips up. I am more engrossed by the faces of the two old ladies who are trotting down the corridor at the time. By the cringe! There are only about half a dozen people on the train and two of them have to be passing at a moment like this. One of them turns away so fast I think her nut is going to twist off. That must be it. A quick trip to the guard and I will be spending the next four months in the chokey for indecent exposure. What a bleeding marvellous way to arrive in the old country. Sir Giles is going to be really chuffed and I can just see the welcome I will get from mum and dad—not that their behaviour on the Isla de Amor was anything to write to the Archbishop of Canterbury about.

"Pull it down!" I yelp.

"I'm moving as fast as I can, darling."

"I mean the blind!"

"Look, no panties."

"I did notice."

"Isn't Timmy lovely, Nat?"

"Gollumptious, Nan."

"He looks good enough to eat."

"You took the words right out of my fevered imagination."

"Oh no," I gasp as they press me down under the combined weight of their bodies.

"For God's sake pull down the blind."

At last one of them reaches behind her and does as I ask and I must confess that there are worse ways to travel. With those two birds browsing over my flesh I feel like an aniseed ball that has been chucked over the wall of Battersea Dog's Home. Two hands are better than one—and four! Well, I will let your imagination develop muscles thinking of the merry tricks we get up to in that compartment. Would you believe that one girl could hang from the rack while the other—no, it sounds too far-fetched, doesn't it? Not the kind of thing that a couple of refined tarts who went to Cheltenham Ladies' College would get up to. But believe me, mateys, not every bird you meet with callouses

13

on her hand got them from digging her old man's vegetable patch.

"Now do it to me, Timmy. Oh, Timmy, Timmy, Timmy. That's heaven. I'd like to have my own private chuffer train so we could do this all the time."

Do that and I will pray for a bleeding rail strike every week, I think to myself. I don't know how I keep pace with them, really I don't. Maybe it has something to do with the fact that I don't really fancy them. I mean, they are fantastic birds looks-wise, but there is something so brazen about them that it can never be anything more than a straightforward up and downer. I find it very easy to poke birds when I give my old man his head and let him get on with it—as I have said, he does that most of the time anyway. It is when my mind starts to reckon a bird as well that it begins to foul up my natural impulses. It happened with a bird called Liz I used to go with when I was cleaning windows. I was on the point of marrying her when my poxy brother-in-law Sid introduced her to his nasty and put the kibosh on everything. You know, I was really stretched to get anywhere with that bird. And all because I fancied her too much. Beats anything you read in the Reader's Digest doesn't it? Oh well, please yourself.

Anyway, there I am putting up a fantastic fight on the floor of the 10.42 when suddenly the ticket collector lights upon the scene—as they say in the teenage romances. To be honest, I regard him as an angel of mercy because I am on the point of surrender. A man can take so much, but giving it is another matter.

"What do you think you're doing?" he says, all taken aback and disgusted.

The two miserable old crones are craning over his shoulder photographing every inch of flesh for their memory banks.

I feel like telling the bloke that if he does not know what we are doing he would do well to consult one of the many manuals available from reputable bookshops or consider entering a monastery. Either that or find out what his old

14

woman gets up to when she tells him she is going out to tree-felling classes.

But I don't. Mainly because I am in a position which makes speech rather difficult.

"We're screwing, you prick," says Nan. "Why don't you get back to your cell and take those two leering slag heaps with you?"

"You want to watch your tongue, young lady," says the stalwart servant of British Rail sternly. I was about to say the same thing, but for a different reason.

"Throw off your serge and live," says Nat whose principles go a bit deeper than Nan's (e.g. more than the standard six inches). "Liberate yourself! Remove your serf rags! This is the only union worth joining."

I don't fancy this joker joining us because he is definitely not the type of person I would invite to any gang bang I was thinking of attending. That is the thing about group sex. It is not the birds I worry about. It is the other blokes. Very nasty!

But luckily I don't have to worry. Our new friend is definitely not interested in participating.

"I am going to have to ask you for your names and addresses," he says haughtily.

Blimey! Here we go. Hardly an hour in the country and I'm halfway to the nick already.

In the background the old birds are twittering away about how they knew this would happen once the socialists nationalised the railways and it is obvious they have not had such a good time since they poked an Empire Loyalist in the goolies with an umbrella at the Conservative Conference of 1952.

"If you don't piss off," says Nan. "I'll go and do something unmentionable in the First Class dining car."

I must say that they are a remarkable couple of birds because they actually get the poor sod to push off on condition that we will give him our addresses when we have got our clothes on. The old birds don't like this at all but nothing short of instant birching would really satisfy them. I hope I don't get quite so vicious when I am that

15

age. Still, with a few more like Nat and Nan about I don't reckon I stand a chance of getting past thirty.

Having a teeny-weeny criminal record for lead-nicking when I was an easily contaminated youth I am not keen to give my name and address to anyone, and have been known to fill in a false monicker on the stubs of raffle tickets. I am therefore relieved that I get my trousers on just as the chuffer pulls into Rugby. Wasting no time I zip up my credentials and grab my suitcase.

"Well, girls," I say. "Nice knowing you. Give my regards to Sir Giles. I'll come round and collect my bonus. Do me a favour and don't mention Funfrall to Punchy, will you?"

"You're not running away?"

"Living to fight another day. It sounds better."

"But Uncle Gilesy will take care of everything. We won't drop you in it. Honestly we won't."

"I know you mean well, girls, but I also know how things can go wrong. That was how I landed in the nick last time."

"You have a criminal record. How super!"

"Yeah. Longer than Ravel's Bolero. Now, I must be off."

The thought of me being Public Enemy Number One obviously turns them on like a fire hose and I have a real job to get out of the door before the train pulls out.

"We'll see you, Timmy!" they holler. "Remember! Screw for peace!"

I wish they had not said that because I get a few very old-fashioned glances from the rest of the people on the platform. This is bad enough but worse is to come. On the way to the buffet, I bump into the two old harpies who were having a butchers at our love fest. I am surprised that they can recognise my face but there is no doubt that it is firmly emblazened on their memories. They both turn the colour of pillar boxes and grab each other's arms. Never slow to give total offence I plunge my hand into my trouser pocket and wait for their eyes to roll across the platform.

"Have you got a two-penny piece for two pennies?" I say eventually withdrawing my pandy, and watch their faces relax into apoplexy. I hop off sharpish before they start any agro and get the next train with a cup of char and a wad

16

inside me. By the cringe, but it is exotic fare that British Rail dish up for you these days. The bloke in front of me complains because the sultanas in his bun are dead flies. "Dey was fresh in today, man," says the loyal servant of the Raj who provides for him. I still don't know if he is referring to the flies.

I get back to Paddington about four o'clock and then it is the last stage of my journey back to Scraggs Lane. I had considered going straight to my penthouse flat in Park Lane but decided that it would break mother's heart if she did not see me right away. England, home and duty.

I am a bit uneasy about seeing mum again after her behaviour with that bearded old nut in the Isla de Amor. I mean, this permissive society bit is all right for people of our age, but your own mother! Frankly, I find it disgusting. I mean, I would not set dad up on a pederast but he is her husband. Gallivanting about in the woods with some naked geezer is not my idea of how my mum should behave—even if she is on holiday. Of course, I blame the papers myself. All these stupid old berks read about the things young people are supposed to be doing and decide to grab themselves a slice of the action before it is too late.

Dad, I can understand. It was no surprise to find him in that woman's hut and I was amazed it took him so long to burn the camp down. I would have thought that he would have packed a can of kerosene with his knotted handkerchief, poured it over the first building he came to and wouf! The whole bleeding thing over in one quick, simple gesture. But mum, she was a surprise. I don't think I will ever get over that.

"Hello Timmie love!"

It is my sister Rosie who opens the door which is another surprise. Rosie behaved with the lack of restraint that characterises the normal English rose on holiday and her relationship with the singing wop, one Ricci Volare—and you don't want more than one, believe me—was hardly what you might call platonic—even if you knew what it meant.

In other words, the two Lea ladies had let the side down

something rotten. Like justice they had not only been done but seen to be done.

Rosie is married to my brother-in-law, Sidney Noggett, once my partner in a humble window-cleaning business, now an aspiring and perspiring business tycoon—or maybe it should be typhoon if that means a big wind—with Funfrall Enterprises who you know about.

"Where's mum?" I ask.

"Standing on her head against the wall."

"She's what?"

"She's taken up yoga."

"Oh blimey."

"Yes. She wants to find herself. Reveal the complete woman."

"I've just left two like that. She's all right, is she?" I tap my nut.

"Oh yeah. She says some bloke on the island put her on to it."

"Oh my gawd. He hasn't shown up has he?"

"No, of course not. What is the matter with you?"

"Nothing, nothing. It just doesn't seem like mum, that's all."

"I think the holiday really did something for her. They say travel broadens the mind, you know."

"Yeah. You can say that again. I think I'm going to stay at home for a bit."

As she talks, Rosie's eyes begin to glaze over and I reckon she is thinking of Mr. Nausea.

"I thought it was marvellous out there. The heat, the different people you met—"

"How's Sid?" I say hurriedly. I mean, I am not president of his fan club, but I do reckon you have got to stick up for your own flesh and blood. Once Clapham's answer to Paul Newman starts getting two-timed, then what hope is there for the rest of us? Into the Common Market and—boom! boom!—hordes of blooming dagos leaving wine glass stains all over your old lady. That is not nice, is it? On the evidence of mum and Rosie you might as well forget about birds and start carving models of the Blackpool Tower out of chicken bones. Of course, it may just have been the weather. Get your average Eyetie or Spaniard over here and his charms probably shrivel up before he has half-filled his hot water bottle.

"He's upstairs," she says. "Recovering."

"Recovering?"

From what? I ask myself. I knew he was having a big thing with this bird on the island, but she looked a very hygienic lady to me. I mean, I cannot believe that she had—

"You can see·him in a minute."

"Oh God. What's he doing here? Why isn't he lording it back at your country house in Streatham?"

"We've sold it."

"Sold it?"

"Yeah, you can talk to him about that an' all. Do you want to see Mum?"

"Naturally."

I follow Rosie through to the front room—which has not changed, right down to my knee marks on the fireside rug —and there is Mum. I would have had difficulty recognising her because she is indeed standing on her head with her feet resting against the wall. Her dentures are on the carpet in front of her head like some kind of name plate.

"Hello ma," I say. "It's me, Timmy. Glad to see you get your knickers from Marks and Sparks. How's it going then?"

Quite a warm greeting from an only son, locked from his mother's eyes through five long weeks, I am certain you will agree. I look down at the carpet for signs of tear stains beginning to appear but I am disappointed.

"Timmy love, never interrupt me when I'm meditating. There are some fish fingers in the fridge."

And that is all I get. Talk about the younger generation. It is the older generation I am worrying about.

"I'd better see Sid then, I suppose. What's the matter with him?"

"He was shot trying to escape from a prisoner of war camp."

"Oh yeah, very funny." You have to hand it to Rosie,

19

she is getting a whole new sense of humour. Very satirical.

"I was shot trying to escape from a prisoner of war camp," says Sid when I ask him.

"It was one of Slat's ideas. You know he was mad keen on the Blitz and starting holiday camps in deserted tube stations with sirens and muzac by courtesy of World War II?"

"I remember something about it."

"Well, that was just the beginning. When he really thought about it, he came up with Prisoner of War Camps. When you settled up for your holiday you were issued with a rank according to how much you had paid. For two hundred quid you could be C.O. It didn't make any bloody difference to the food you got but people are crazy about status, aren't they? Instead of Holiday Hosts you had guards and that cut down on the organisation because they didn't organise games. They just tried to stop you escaping. Every intake was given a spade and a pair of wire clippers and there was a prize at the end of the fortnight for who got farthest."

"How did you get shot?"

"To get a bit of publicity at the beginning, they got a real German prison camp guard. Well, you know what the Krauts are like. Very thorough. They like to give value for money. I was trying to whip up a bit of enthusiasm for an assault on the electrified fence and he shot me."

"He might have killed you!"

"He said he was doing it for my own good. You see the fence really was electrified. Slattery reckoned that some dodgy bugger could take advantage and get his two weeks for nothing if you didn't deincentivize him."

"Didn't what?"

"It's a word I learnt on one of Funfrall's bleeding courses. You can have it. I'm not going to need it any more."

"Have you been invalided out?"

"I've resigned with honour."

"Why Sid? You were doing so well."

"Breathing is what I do best, Timmo, and I want to make

a career of it. My next posting was going to be Kew Gardens."

"Kew Gardens!"

"Yes. They wanted to get Malaysia but Eye Twang Knickers, or whatever his name is, wouldn't play ball. You see, Timmo, when my number nearly came up they got more applications from people who wanted to be guards than prisoners. It's understandable when you think about it, you know what I mean? Much more fun machine-gunning people and setting guard dogs on them than it is digging bleeding tunnels. Sir Giles saw that straight away. First of all, he tried to get the Japs to start another Death Railway and promised them cheap labour—but they thought it would be bad for their car exports so in the end he had to settle for the Hot House at Kew. Two bananas and a survival pack is four hundred guineas with cremation at the crematorium of your choice thrown in for nothing. Up on the cat walk with your Hirohito forage cap and a Nippon issue rifle is six hundred guineas or you can have the intermediate, 'Jungle Boy' holiday, Dyak blow pipe and a plastic shrunken head for every camper you knock off. Personally, I thought it was going a bit too far. Specially when they said I was going to be umpire. I mean, get a few light ales in that lot and they'd open up on anything. So I said bugger it and handed in my armband."

"So you've jacked it in, Sid?"

"Precisely."

"Going to leave you a bit short, isn't it?"

"Well, I thought of that, didn't I? I told Sir Giles straight. I said 'you can't go around having your senior executives shot by blood-crazed Krauts and expect to leave a nice taste in everybody's mouth.'"

"Right, Sid."

"Especially if they are reading about it in the News of the People. I mean, it gets around."

"You were approached were you, Sid?"

"Not exactly approached, Timmy. But I have a few contacts. Know what I mean?"

"Oh yeah. So Sir Giles paid up, did he?"

"In a manner of speaking, yes, Timmo. What he really did was to indemnify me against the enormity of the mental and physical suffering I had endured in the course of pursuing my duties in a manner calculated to further enhance the unbesmirched reputation of Funfrall Enterprises."

"Blimey Sid, did you say all that?"

"No, Timmy, my solicitor did. Very good bloke he is and all. I'll give you an introduction if you ever need one."

Solicitors? Sidney is really beginning to motor. Another couple of weeks and he'll be tearing crumpets with the Queen Mother.

"So you grabbed a nice helping of moola, did you, Sid?"

"Nosey basket, aren't you? Yes, if you must know. I did accept a settlement. But not in cash, mind."

"What, then?"

"I bought a hotel."

CHAPTER TWO

"You done what?"

"I've bought a hotel, Timmo. Very nice article. Down on the south coast. Hoverton, do you know it?"

"Mum took me there for the day once when I was a nipper. Haven't Funfrall got a place near there?"

"Yeah, just outside the town."

"Sid, what I don't understand is why you're buying it. I thought Old Man Slat was going to give you some mazuma."

"Well, he has really. The price is dirt cheap when you think what I'm getting. It's one of these big old Regency places. Funfrall are selling off a lot of their stuff as part of a rationalisation programme. Mind you, it's still costing me a bomb. That's why I sold El Nido."

"And Rosie and the kid are going to live there with you?"

"Not to start with. I want to get the place sorted out first."

"Sounds fantastic, Sid. What kind of shape is it in?"

Sid begins to look uncomfortable. "Quite good, I think. I haven't seen it yet."

"Haven't seen it?"

"Well, you know what Sir Giles is like. He came up with the idea so fast; and he was so enthusiastic, I thought it would sound rude if I started humming and haing."

"You didn't worry about humming and haing when he suggested that you got your head shot off in the Hot House at Kew. I bet he came up with that idea pretty fast, too."

"I've seen some photographs," says Sid pathetically. "It looks very nice." He pulls open a bedside drawer and thrusts a couple of crumpled prints into my hand.

"Blimey, that bird is wearing a crinoline, isn't she? I didn't know they had invented cameras in those days. Haven't you got anything a bit more recent?"

The photographs Sid has given me are khaki coloured and have horse-drawn bathing cabins in the foreground. Sometimes I think that Sid has more luck than judgement.

"Anything that is bricks and mortar is worth its weight in gold these days," says Sid sulkily. "I've got the freehold, you know."

"What does that mean?"

Sid is relieved to find that he can assert himself again. "It means, you prick, that I own it. I am not renting it."

"Well, good luck, Sid. I'm certain you'll do very well. Not exactly your line, though, is it?"

"No really new opportunity is ever likely to be, is it?"

"True, Sid. What am I going to do at Funfrall, now that you're gone?"

Sid takes a sip at his Robinson's Lemon Barley Water and gives me his "I don't really know what it means but I am trying to appear inscrutable" look.

"I've been think about that," he says. In the old days, I would have thrown myself full length and kissed the end of his pyjama cord saying: "Oh, Sid am I deceiving myself when I think that you might actually be offering me the chance of employment in your new passport to easy riches?—" the last few words being drowned in grateful sobs. Now I am older and wiser.

"What did you have in mind?" I say coolly.

Sidney selects a grape and, attempting to peel it non-

23

chalantly, manages to crush it between finger and thumb so that the gunge runs down the front of his pyjamas. With typical Lea restraint I pretend that I have not noticed this distasteful incident.

"I was thinking," says Sid, scraping the remains of the grape off his chest with a dirty teaspoon, "that you might be able to do yourself a bit of good by coming in with me."

He leans back against the bed like a satisfied dog owner who has just given his pet a new brand of worm powder.

"I remember you saying something like that to me before," I say. "On a couple of occasions. First time I ended up losing the bird I was thinking of getting spliced to and the second—well, I'm not exactly loaded down with gelt, am I?"

"Money isn't everything, Timmo," says my crafty old brother-in-law. "You got some wonderful experience on both occasions—wonderful experiences too. You mustn't try and rush at things. You can't get rich overnight, you know."

"You haven't done too bad, Sid."

"I've had the rub of the green, mate. I'd be the first to admit it. But hard graft has played its part."

"Well graft, anyway."

"I'll pretend I don't understand you. Look, Timmo, I respect you; you've got talent, I need you. Let me put it like that. I've got a feeling the Cromby—"

"The what?!!"

"The Cromby—that's the name of the hotel—could be a real bonanza."

"Not with a name like that, it can't."

"I agree. How about the Hoverton Country Club?"

"I thought it was on the sea front?"

"Yeah, well it is, but the public gardens are just round the corner."

"Come off it, Sid. That isn't going to fool anybody twice."

"How about the Ritz-Carlton?"

"No, Sid."

"The Hoverton Hilton?"

24

"Sid!"

"The Noggett?"

"Do me a favour. I prefer the Cromby to that."

"Yeah, well, that's not really important. We can worry about the name later. What I want to find out is whether you're interested or not."

"I thought I had a wonderful future mapped out for me with Funfrall?"

"You did as long as I was there. I'd have seen you alright, Timmo. Like I always try to do. But I have to take the broader view. I weighed everything up and I reckoned that this was the right time to make a move. With a hotel we can concentrate on the right section of the holiday trade—the bleeders with money. You could get old before your time running round those chalets all day."

"You're right there, Sid."

"Of course I'm right. Look, I tell you what, Timmo. If you help me make a go of this place, I'll put you in as manager when we buy another one. How about that? That's handsome, isn't it?"

"Very handsome, Sid. Alright, I'm on."

"Good thinking, Timmo, you won't regret it."

"I'll remember you saying that, Sid."

"You do that, you do that. Well, I suppose I'd better try and get a little rest now. Tell mum I fancy a spot of that chicken broth, will you?"

"She's standing on her head in the front room."

"Oh, well, Rosie then."

"Was it serious, Sid?"

"What? Oh, my injury you mean? No, Timmo, none of my moving parts. Nothing that Rosie has missed yet. I reckon a spot of sea air is just what I need to convalesce." The way he winks at me makes me think that Sid is becoming more like his old self again.

I pad downstairs to find Dad standing in the hall. As he sees me his face splits into a broad scowl.

"You back then, are you?" he grunts.

"Right in one, Dad. Nothing wrong with your eyes."

"Don't take the micky out of me, sonny Jim. How long

are you staying for? This place isn't a bleeding hotel, you know."

"I would never have noticed if it hadn't been for the length of time it took me to get room service. Come off it dad, this is my home, you know. I'm entitled to a few days in the bosom of my family."

"Don't talk dirty. Your mother's in the next room."

"Still standing on her head, is she? You want to watch it. If all the blood runs out of her feet she'll have to walk on her knees."

"Bleeding Sidney as well. I thought we'd got rid of you lot when the window cleaning business broke up."

"Well, you never know your luck do you? I'm surprised to hear you say that about Sidney after that smashing holiday he organised for you."

"Smashing holiday? I don't call that no smashing holiday. I've only just got my stomach straight again."

"That must have been very difficult, dad."

"Don't take the piss. You always did have too much lip. All that wog food. Dirty bastards they are. I had enough of that during the war. Nearly killed me."

"Well, mum enjoyed it, dad."

"Don't talk to me about that, neither. It turned your mother crackers. It was the sun done that. Melted her brain. Bloody Yogi."

"Yoga, dad."

"I don't care what it is. It's not right. Woman of her age. Disgusting."

"Everyody needs an interest in life, dad."

"She's got me. I'm her interest in life."

"Maybe she's meditating about you now, dad."

"I want my supper, not bleeding meditation."

That reminds me that Sid wants his chicken broth so I push into the kitchen where Rosie is helping little Jason to feed himself. The sight of all those little tins of vomit being smeared round his cake-hole is so disgusting that it even surpasses the horror of mum's scarlet mush when she staggers through the door. She looks like a hollowed-out turnip with a two-hundred watt bulb inside it.

All in all, I am more than relieved when a few days later, I find myself sitting in the passenger seat of Sidney's Rover 2000 as we purr along the seafront of Hoverton. As ardent fans will know, I am no stranger to seaside resorts, but definitely not used to speeding about in expensive motor cars. The fact that Sid has been allowed to hang on to his company car really impresses me. We must be on to something good this time.

It is only when we have sped along the sea front for about two miles that I begin to have second thoughts.

"We haven't passed it, have we?" says Sid anxiously.

"Looks as if somebody else has." Sid follows my gaze and his jaw drops faster than a pair of lead knickers.

"Blimey. I see what you mean. Looks more like the Zomby than the Cromby."

Most of the buildings along the front have been tarted up and painted fashionable shades of pink, lemon and blue but the Cromby is peeling like an eight-hour suntan and looks as if it was last painted in order to camouflage it during Zeppelin raids. Even the glass sign is cracked.

"Nice going, Sid," I say. "You struck a shrewd bargain there. He didn't throw in London Bridge as well, did he? If he did you were done because we've sold it to the Yanks."

"Shut up!"

"I like the situation, too. I didn't know they had bomb sites down here. Maybe it's part of a slum clearance scheme."

"I said 'shut up'. I'm thinking."

"Thinking about how long it will take us to get back to London, I hope. If you rang up Sir Giles from the News of the People offices he might give you your money back."

"Don't be so blooming hasty. It's right on the beach."

"On the shingle, Sid. Looks like they get a lot of oil tankers around here, too. And what's that big culvert coming out in the middle of the beach? Niffs a bit, doesn't it?"

"Oh, belt up, you're always moaning. You never take a chance, that's your trouble. If it wasn't for me you'd be working on a bloody building site."

"If I nicked a few bricks we might be able to do something with this place."

27

"Very funny. You're a right little ray of sunshine, aren't you? Come on, let's take a look at it. We've got nothing to lose."

"Don't talk too soon. Do they know you're coming?"

"No, I thought it would be favourite to turn up as if we were ordinary guests. That way we'll get the real feel of the place."

"Good thinking, Sid. Trouble is I reckon I've got the feeling of the place without even going through the doors."

Sid does not say anything but puts his foot down so hard that I am practically on the back seat as we skid to a halt outside the hotel. Sid waits for a moment, presumably to see if anybody comes out to greet us, and then opens the door of the car.

"Right. That's one thing you're going to be able to do something about," he says.

"Whadyermean, Sid? You reckon me for a blooming commissionaire or something?"

"We've all got to play a part," he says. "No skiving about at the beginning."

Marvellous, isn't it? And I thought I was going to start moving up a few rungs. We go through the swing doors and I practically have to hang on to Sid's coat tails it is so dark. Like the Chamber of Horrors only with less character.

"Very restrained, isn't it?" I say.

"Shut up."

The reception area is deserted and I will swear there are cobwebs on the register. Pinned above the desk is a poster stating the films that are on at the Roxie. I remember passing the Roxie on the way to the hotel. It is now a Bingo Hall.

"Perhaps we could take a leaf out of Sir Giles's book and run holidays for those in love with the past," I say. "How about starting off with the Norman invasion?"

"One of the first things I'm going to miss about you is your marvellous sense of humour," says Sid. "Now get some service around here before I do my nut."

I have bashed the bell about three times and am wondering whether the grey stuff on top of the elk's head is dust or dandruff, when an oldish bird with a black dress and matching cardigan comes up some stairs beside the reception. She has thin wispy hair and a twisted jaw that looks as if it has been left out in the rain and got warped. Round her neck is a gold chain to which are attached a pair of specs.

"I'm not deaf," she says irritably. "I'm not deaf."

"I'm sorry," I say. "We would like to book a room."

"You what?"

"We would like to book a room!" The tone of Sid's voice betrays the fact that the Cromby is appearing less of a gold mine than it did a few hours previously. The old bag shuts her book.

"I've told you once," she says. "I'm not deaf. There's no need to shout like that." Sidney makes a big effort and controls himself. "Is it possible for my friend and myself to book a double room—with single beds?"

"What? You'll have to speak up. You're whispering. What is it you want?"

"I'd like an axe," grits Sid.

"What do you want an axe for? Have you come to chop wood? You should have gone round the back."

"Give me strength," says Sid turning away.

"What does he want strength for?" says the elderly nut. "Has he come to chop wood or not? I can't stand temperament. Especially about a little thing like that. Young people today have no staying power."

"We would like to book a room."

"You what?"

"Forget it," says Sid. "I can't understand why I ever thought it was a good idea in the first place. Let's have a bash at the pier and go home."

"You want some rooms," says the old bag. "Why didn't you say so before?"

"It never occurred to me to ask," I say, revealing once again my aptitude for the lowest form of humour.

"We would like our room with two single beds," says Sid pronouncing each word like one of those birds on "Parlez-vous francais?".

"Oh?" Madam looks us up and down and it suddenly

29

occurs to me that she thinks we are a couple of poufdahs. The very idea!

"He's my brother," says Sid.

"Oh, well I suppose that's alright." She does not sound very convinced. "Do you want a bathroom?"

"No thanks," says Sid. "The sight of him naked might inflame my fevered imagination to the point where the floodgates burst and I be carried away in a maelstrom of primitive lust."

"Just a basin, then?"

"That should prove very adequate. What time is supper?"

"Dinner," she stresses the word, "is from six forty-five to seven thirty."

"Very continental," I observe to Sid. "Gives you all of fifteen minutes to get the sand out of your plimsoles."

"We find that most of our guests like to be finished in time for Coronation Street."

"I can imagine," says Sid. "The solid chomp of gnashers battling against the clock—"

"The best seats in the tele lounge filling up from seven fifteen onwards."

"The latecomers wiping the blancmange from their tuxedos as they struggle for the last two chairs."

"It's not like that at all," says the Lady in Black coldly as she settles her specs on the end of her nose. "Perhaps you would be good enough to sign the register."

"What about our cases?" Sid indicates the door.

"I'm afraid Mr. Martin is recovering from a hernia operation." She raises her eyes towards the ceiling on the word "hernia" as if averting them from a blue photograph.

"He's the hall porter, I suppose?"

"That is correct."

"And may I inquire what your name is?"

"Miss Primstone."

"I should have guessed. Well, if we get our cases perhaps you can show us where our room is."

I wish Sid had not said that because the minute the words

have passed his lips, a much better guide appears patting her jet black curls into place.

"Sorry I'm late, Miss Primstone," says the newcomer not sounding at all sorry. "But we lost a couple of balls in the long grass and I stayed behind to look for them." I can see a piece of straw sticking out of her hair so I have no reason to disbelieve her. She has big tits and big eyes which roll all over Sid and me while she is talking. I decide that I have fallen desperately in love with her body.

"You should have left them there," snaps Miss P. "Five o'clock is when you're supposed to come on duty."

"Yes Miss Primstone." Miss P. turns to select a key and the bird sticks her tongue out at her and winks at us.

"We must have a game some time," says Sid. "Golf, is it?"

"No, tennis. Are you any good?"

"I'm a bit rusty at the moment. Haven't played seriously for years."

I have never heard such a load of balls. If you gave Sid a tennis racket he would think it was for straining chips.

"Oh, that's alright. I'm only just starting."

"I'm Sidney Noggett, and this is my brother-in-law Timothy Lea."

"Pleased to meet you. I'm Sandra."

"Hello Sandra."

This bird is definitely one of those who carries an invisible banner which has "I like sex" written all over it. She moves as if she is very conscious of her body and she keeps licking her lips and patting her hair. I find that highly strung birds of that type really lap up the sack work. My thoughts are interrupted by Sidney coming the senior partner.

"Get the cases in, Timmy, will you?" he says, sliding out his cigarette case and resting his elbow nonchalantly on the counter.

"Yas sah Massa Noggett," I say in my best Brixton accent. "To hear is to obey."

When I come in again, Sandra is behind the counter and Miss Primstone is drawing her cardigan around herself protectively. "We're having a little trouble with the heating," she says. "You may find it takes a few moments for the hot water to come through."

In practice, it takes three days but that is not the first thought that occurs to me when we are shown to our room. It looks like the inside of a mahogany packing case, and it is only possible to stand upright just inside the door.

"People must have been a lot smaller when this place was built," I say.

"We have never had any complaints."

"Probably because people bash their heads on the ceiling and get their mouths jammed shut," murmurs Sid.

"If you don't like the room, I am certain there are other hotels in Hoverton which would be capable of providing accommodation."

It is amazing how the old bag can hear when you don't want her to. I reckon I am going to like the place a lot more when she has left.

"No offence intended," says Sid. "Just my little joke."

Miss Primstone gives Sid a look that suggests she does not like jokes in any size and goes out slamming the door behind her.

"What did you say you were going to call this place? The Ritz-Carlton? It's more like the blitzed Carlton."

I sit down on one of the beds and the springs make a disastrous creaking sound like someone biting through thirty wafers in one go.

"Is that a damp patch on the wall or haircream?"

I don't get a chance to answer because the door suddenly opens and the second bit of good news that day bundles over the threshold. She is small and blonde and wearing a little black dress and a cap like an upturned tennis vizor.

"Oh, sorry ever so," she says in a squeaky cockney voice. "I just popped in to turn down the beds."

She looks as if she has never turned down beds in her life and I can see Sidney's mind travelling down the same well-worn route as my own.

"Be my guest," he purrs. "Have you worked here long?"

"It seems like a long time," says the girl, "but I suppose it's only been about five weeks."

"Business good?"

"Not very. There's one or two old people who live here all the time. Retired, you know. Then there's the commercials and the other old people who come here because they can't afford anything better."

"No young people?"

"Young people? You must be joking, dear. There's the odd bit of stolen lust, I suppose, but most young people wouldn't touch this place with a barge pole. You and your —your friend are the youngest we've got at the moment."

"He's my brother-in-law."

The maid looks relieved. "Oh good. We get a few of those as well, you know."

"You live on the premises?"

"What do you want to know for?" There is more hope than irritation in her voice.

"Oh, I just thought if I wanted a sleeping pill or something, you might be able to help me."

"Cheeky devil!" She puts her hand to her mouth and giggles.

"I hope your bed doesn't creak like this one?" I throw in.

"Oh, you are awful!"

"I wasn't suggesting anything."

"Not half, you weren't."

"We both have a bit of trouble sleeping, don't we Timmy?"

"You know what I reckon might be good for that, Sidney?"

"No, Timmo?"

"Ooh! I'm not going to listen to another word. Wait 'til I tell my friend Audrey about you two."

"Does she work here, too?"

"She shares a room with me."

"Oh!"

"Now don't you start getting any ideas. It may be our evening off but we don't go flaunting ourselves with just anybody, you know."

"I didn't know you knew anybody we know."

"What?"

"It doesn't matter. What does Audrey look like? Is she pretty like you?"

"Flattery will get you anywhere—within reason."

"Why don't we all go out and have a little drink later? I'd suggest supper but we've got a bloke who may be joining us here about seven-fifteen, so we'll be eating in."

"Shall I see if I can find someone for him?"

"No, no, that won't be necessary. We're doing a bit of business with him, that's all. I'm not even certain he's going to show up."

I am bloody certain he is not going to show up. Sid can be a cunning bastard sometimes especially when it is a question of keeping his wallet shut. I have known oncers to crumble with age when they eventually emerge into the light.

"I hope you're going to like Audrey," I say when we have sent our little squeaking friend on her way.

"What do you mean? I'm having that one. June, or whatever her name was."

"Sidney, really. It was obvious that the girl was insane about me. She couldn't keep her eyes off me."

"Don't be daft. She felt sorry for you, that's all. She was humouring you. She prefers the older, more sophisticated type. I can tell. You latch on to her mate and cross your fingers that she doesn't fancy me as well."

It occurs to me that this is not like the Sidney Noggett who was warning me off the frippet when I was applying for a job as a Holiday Host, and I find it impossible not to comment on this fact.

"You're changing your tune a bit, aren't you, Sid? You didn't used to approve of fraternising with the staff. And what about Rosie?"

"Out of sight, out of mind," says Sid tapping one of his mince pies. "What the eye doesn't see the heart doesn't worry about." You are dead right there, I think to myself, wondering how much Sid's vanity will allow him to imagine of what was going on between Rosie and Ricci Volare— precious little, I should think. "It was different when I was at Funfrall anyway. I had more of a position to keep up. I feel I've shed a few of my cares. Know what I mean?"

"Yes, Sid."

"After all, I am supposed to be convalescing down here. It's in Rosie's interest if I can check that the equipment is up to scratch."

"Very thoughtful of you, Sid."

"I thought you'd see it that way. And don't get any ideas about putting the screws on me with Rosie, will you? You do and your prospects go straight up the creek. And I don't just mean your job ones, either."

Sid is no doubt remembering how I applied pressure when I discovered him having a flutter in the tool shed with the bird I was about to offer a wedding ring for the same services. Still, that was a couple of years ago, before moral values had been completely eroded, and when there was no prospect of a hotel management to seal my outraged lips. I assure Sid that I have a complete understanding of his meaning, and we go down to the cocktail lounge for a quick snifter before supper.

The bloke behind the bar has receding hair flattened against his head as if by a great, greasy wind and his forehead is corrugated like a perished rubber mask. Behind bushy eyebrows lurk evil darting eyes and his teeth look like a job lot rummaged from a vet's dustbin. Just to gaze at his mush is to wonder whether the bar sells Rennies.

"You gave me a start, gentlemen," he says pushing something under the counter hurriedly. I would like to give him three miles' start and then piss off in the opposite direction, but one must not be too unkind.

"Large Scotch, please," says Sid. "And what are you going to have, Timmo? Half of bitter? Half of bitter, please."

I was about to say that a large Scotch would slide down very nicely but you have to move fast when Sid is in the chair.

"Fairly quiet, is it?" says Sid adding a dash of water to his Scotch. I am pleased to see that he also gets two dead flies, a mosquito and an insect I have not seen before.

Whatever it is, the barman looks up at the ceiling as he retrieves it, so it seems to have been a resident.

"Sorry about that, Sir. The boy must have forgotten to change it. You can't get the staff now, you know. Yes, it is very quiet but this isn't our busy time. We do a lot of business in the autumn. It's amazing how many hotel people come here for a holiday when their own season is over."

"Must give them a tremendous feeling of confidence," says Sid holding up his glass to the light. "Have you got one with a more neutral shade of lipstick on it? This is a bit overpowering for me."

"Sorry about that, Sir. The girl should have seen to that."

I can see that Sid is dying to get his hands round the little jerk's neck and tell him who is the new lord and master but he manages to control himself.

"You are the barman, though, aren't you?"

"Head Barman."

"How many more are there?"

"I'm the only one at the moment. We will be taking some more on, later in the summer. Students, probably."

"Good," says Sid. "Have you been here long?"

"Eighteen years. Only the receptionist, Miss Primstone, has been here longer than that. Oh, and of course, the cook."

"Why did you say 'of course'?"

"Oh, well, Mrs. Caitley is something of an institution around here. She is practically part of the hotel."

"I hope she is nothing like this part," says Sid, fishing something else out of his glass.

Before weasel-features can apportion the blame there is an ear-piercing shriek from the vestibule which makes me choke on my beer.

"Talk of the devil," mutters the barman under his breath.

I am about to ask for further details when the room is filled by a large, red lady holding her clenched fists before her in the manner of someone doing one of the exercises from the Charles Atlas Course. Not that this baby looks as if anybody is going to kick sand in her face. She pushes

36

her way to the bar and pours a generous slug of brandy into a tumbler.

"That's it," she hollers at a pitch that would make Maria Callas rush out for a throat spray. "I can't go on! Either he goes or I go. I don't mind the nig nogs. I don't mind the equipment—though it's rotten!" She bangs her glass down and half its contents jump across the bar; a loss which is speedily made good—"it's him!!!"

"It's the head waiter she's on about," whispers the barman. "They don't see eye to eye."

"Nobody tells me how to cook," snarls Big Red giving me a hint that she is not the Phantom of the Opera in drag. "Nobody ever has, and nobody ever will."

While she is looking at the ceiling over the rim of her glass, a thin, effeminate man wearing a dinner jacket rushes in. He is wringing his hands as if he hopes to extract water from them.

"Calm yourself, Mrs. Caitley," he squeals. "Calm yourself. Think of the guests." The last sentence causes an enormous shudder to run through Mrs. Caitley like an earth tremor in a raspberry jelly.

"I would beg to inform you," she says icily, "that thinking about the guests has been my one pre-occupation throughout twenty years in the hotel business."

"And I can assure you, dear lady, that I have no less a desire to serve the best interests of our patrons."

"Don't you 'dear lady' me, you odious pipsqueak."

As heads begin to pop round the door, Mrs. Caitley picks up a bowl of mildewed peanuts that Sidney has already rejected and begins to hurl them one by one at the head waiter. She is a lousy shot as Sid is quick to find out when he cops one in the eye, but it is an impressive sight, reminding me of one of those big Russian ladies warming up for the discus.

"Good—wholesome—English—fare," she pants as she empties the bowl. "I-will-not-cook-continental-garbage."

"Cor, love-a-duck," says Sid as we cower towards the dining room. "What a blooming carve-up."

"Are they at it again," says Sandra breezily as she bounces past. "Oh, I am sorry."

She does something with her mouth which makes me think of juicy strawberries and I fight an immediate impulse to pull her down behind the reception desk.

"Let's nip out for a cup of cha and a wad," I say as I peer into the dining room.

"No," says Sid firmly. "We're going to see this through."

The dining room is the darkest room yet and I expect to see a coffin lying on a couple of trestles in the middle of it. One reason for the gloom is probably the state of the table cloths which look like the ones that were not washed in New Wonder Sudso. The menu holders are curling at the edges and mine has a dead fly behind its acetate sleeve. The Cromby is very hot on flies.

The main thing that strikes you about the menu is that although all the dishes are printed in French this has been crudely crossed out in Biro, and an English equivalent put beside each entry. Thus "Potage Creme Royale" becomes "Brown Windsor Soup" and "Petit poissons au style Portugaise sur pain grillé" appears as "Sardines on Toast!" In this it is not difficult to see the hand of the dreaded Mrs. Caitley. You don't have to be good at doing crosswords to know that she likes the frog-loving head waiter less than wire-wool knickers.

That creature comes across the floor at a fast mince like a ballet dancer about to launch himself into full flutter. He is patting his hair and throwing his head back and has obviously been through an ab-so-lute-ly ghast-ly experience in the cocktail lounge.

"So sorry about that aw-ful scene," he squeals. "Now, have you decided what you'd like? The veal is a dream today. I made the sauce myself and it is quite, quite delicious—though I say it as shouldn't."

He gives us the kind of smile which immediately makes you look out of the window and Sid and I order the soup and mixed grill.

"This place gives me the creeps, Sid," I say when Superpouf has pushed off. "You want to turn it into a sanatorium

38

or get rid of everybody and start from scratch."

"Dodgy, Timmy. I don't have the training for your first caper, and if I bring a quack in I'll have to surrender some of my control. Also, there's too much capital investment in equipment. Your second alternative appeals to me but I can't chuck the whole bleeding lot of them out in one go. The place has got to keep functioning. It's going to be my livelihood, remember. Yours too. No. What we've got to do is winkle them out one by one and replace them with reliable people. Also, we want it to be their idea that they should go. Redundancy payments would cripple me with some of these buggers. They were practically born in the broom closets."

"You really think about it, don't you Sid?" I say admiringly. I mean, he is a shit-heap, but you have to hand it to him for applied villainy.

"Got to, Timmo," says Sid smugly. "That's one thing my experience with Slat taught me. You've got to cover all the angles."

I consider asking if having a butchers at the property he was considering buying could be considered as one of the angles but decided against it. There is no point in sullying our relationship with verbal agro at this stage.

The food, when it comes, is not as bad as I had expected. Bad, but no worse than my mum dishes out. When you have tasted my mum's grub then you have tasted nothing. The only seasoning she knows about is the three after spring. Rosie gave her a cookery book one Christmas and she used it to prop up the wonky leg on the dresser. That is probably why I am so generous about Mrs. Caitley's efforts. You could float a pepper pot on the brown windsor soup and the peas should have been served with a blow-pipe, but the mixed grill is quite tasty once you put the worcester sauce to work on it and I have no complaint about the chips.

"Do you fancy the Bombe Surprise?" I say to Sid who is looking around for the drinks we ordered at the beginning of the meal.

"I'd like to drop one on that bloody wine waiter," he says. "The service in this place is diabolical."

By the time the bloke does come we are into the coffee and Sid tells him to piss off and bring us a couple of brandies.

"That's going to be one of the good things about this job. We should be able to get stuck into some very nice nosh once we get the place sorted out."

"Amongst other things," I say as I watch June and what is presumably Audrey, tripping past for our little rendez-vous. "I'm glad you decided you wanted June."

Sid looks up and his face when he sees Audrey is a real study. This bird is a knockout and she gives us both a long, cool look which demonstrates real interest. She has long shoulder-length black hair and a sultry expression which makes me think she probably scratches. I down my brandy so quickly that I get prickles up my nose.

"Don't want to keep them waiting, do we?" I say, starting to get up.

"Timmo. *Please!* I thought you were beginning to understand what it's all about. Never appear too eager. Surely you know that?"

"Yeah, Sid. Sorry. I just wanted to get out of this place, that's all."

As if overhearing me, Superpouf zooms to our side and fixes me with an engaging smile. This bloke really has it all. Head cocked on one side, hand dangling limply from the wrist.

"Can I have your room number, please. You are to-gether, aren't you?"

"Yes, but we're just good friends," says Sid brusquely. "One two seven."

"If you've bought the bleeding hotel I don't know why we didn't have separate rooms," I say, as the Nancy with the laughing eyes trips off to wield his ballpoint.

"We should have done but I just didn't think of it. I'm so used to being skint that I forget sometimes."

"I've noticed."

"Don't be cheeky. Remember who's the gaffer round here. Right, now let's go and sort out those birds. You take what

40

you can get, all right? And don't let on who we are. Say we're sales reps, O.K.?"

"What are we flogging?"

"Cars. That sounds as if it's got some money in it. Now, come on."

Three hours later we are standing outside the back door of the hotel in a fine drizzle and trying to decide on our next move. Both the girls are hopelessly pissed and my judgement is not exactly faultless. Amongst other things, we have been ten-pin bowling, in which Sid got his finger stuck in the ball and nearly said goodbye to it. I will always remember him doing this great wind-up and then following the ball for the first ten yards down the alley. For a wonderful moment I thought he was going to overtake it and be the first man to make a strike with his own body.

We have also lost a fortune in small change—all mine, of course—on the pin-table machines on the pier. Very few of them seem to be working although they have no problem in gobbling up 5p pieces.

We have also done a great deal of boozing and I now think I know the inside of every pub in Hoverton. Sid has taken me out to the kasi and we have agreed that he can have first crack in our room while I nip upstairs. The bird situation is no problem because neither of us has any preference. June does seem to fancy Sid and Audrey has only drawn the line when I tried to stroke her tits in the public bar of "The Three Jolly Matelots". That was when I decided I must take the water cure. Swill down as much as you can and it dilutes the alcohol. I don't want to fall down on the job with an acute attack of brewer's droop.

"Where's your key, June? Can't you get it out?"

This salty sally reduces both girls to parrot schisms of mirth and I am soaked to the skin before the door is eventually unlocked.

"Bloody marvellous hotels where they lock the front door at eleven," moans Sid.

"You should be grateful. Saves you a lot of embarrassment. It isn't going to do your reputation much good if the

41

new owner is seen testing his tonk on every skivvy in the place."

"You're a silver-tongued bastard, aren't you?" Sid slips his arm round June's waist and we all stand there making "sshhssh" noises at each other. There is hardly a light on in the place and only the horrible smell tells me that we must be near the kitchens.

I take Audrey in my arms for a warm-up snog near the foot of the stairs and press her back against the door of what turns out to be a broom cupboard. I learn this fact when we slowly topple into a welter of vacuum cleaners and tins of floor polish. Maybe I should have had some more water. When we struggle out, Sidney and June have disappeared and all I can hear is the hall clock ticking. God knows where the night porter is; not that I particularly want to meet him in my present situation.

"Oh, you're fantastic," I murmur into Audrey's lughole. "Absolutely fantastic." This is Lea's standard Mark I gambit and seldom needs to be followed up with anything more imaginative before the bedsprings start playing "Love's Old Sweet Melody". All birds lap up a diet of non-stop flattery if delivered with sufficient enthusiasm because it backs up their own judgement. They feel both reassured and impressed by your good taste. I know I have said this before but you can't repeat the golden rule too often.

"Go on with you," whispers Audrey. "I bet you say that to all the girls."

"I wish I could," I murmur passionately. "But the words would stick in my throat."

Diabolical, isn't it? But Audrey grabs my hand and practically drags me up the stairs. We get up to the third landing just as Sid is gently shutting the door of our room with June inside it. He gives a little wave and a thumbs-up sign and I hear the bedsprings creaking before I get to the turn in the stairs.

"Are you going to make me a cup of Ovaltine?" I murmur to my sultry companion.

"Something better than that," she says squeezing my thigh. At least, I think she means to squeeze my thigh but

42

the light on the stairs is practically non-existent.

"Don't scream like that!" she hisses. "You'll wake everyone up."

"Watch what you're doing with your hands then," I howl in my anguish. "Otherwise we'll be making this journey for nothing."

By the cringe, but it is big, this hotel. Another couple of flights and I am looking for Sherpa Tensing to hand me an oxygen mask. The only thing that keeps me going is the outline of Audrey's delicious little body before me. Funny how a few days before, I was thinking that I never wanted to see another woman. Now I can hardly wait to get inside that bedroom. I stretch out my hand and run it lightly over her tulip bulb backside. This is the life. Free bed and never bored. She pauses outside a door and presses a finger to her lips. I remove it and we dissolve into a deep kiss. She puts a hand behind my thigh and pulls me towards her savagely. She does not say much, this girl, but her heart is in the right place. The rest of her is not badly situated, either. Just to make sure, I slip my hand up underneath the back of her skirt and am browsing happily as she reaches behind her and turns the knob—the doorknob, I hasten to add, though you could be excused for asking!

I press forward and imagine us doing a slow motion shuffle towards the bed as the door swings open. This is a very beautiful thought and it is therefore doubly choking when I glance inside and see that one of the two beds in the large dog's kennel is already occupied. Occupied is perhaps the wrong word. It has a large naked man lying in it with his tonk flopped on one side, like a boiled leek. He seems to be asleep. Audrey is apparently unaware that she has a guest because she hooks her hand into the waist band of my trousers and starts to pull me into the room.

"Hem, hem," I murmur with the discretion that has made the name Lea synonymous with upper crust gentility (you wouldn't believe I only got "O" level woodwork, would you?). "Did you know you had company?"

That bird spins round and says a few words I have not heard since Nat and Nan were last on the rampage. "Filthy bastard" is the most repeatable phrase she utters.

"A friend of yours?"

"We finished a long time ago. He's taking a terrible liberty."

"Do you want me to throw him out?"

"No. You'd better not. I know! We'll go round to his room. It will serve him right. He can have a nice sleep here."

Phew! Thank goodness for that. For a moment I could see that lovely piece of nookey slipping through my fingers.

"Wait a minute." There is a piece of pink ribbon lying on the dresser and I carefully slip it under the uninvited guest's tonk and tie a floppy bow in it. Call me a romantic if you like, but it is little gestures like that that make the world a happier place to live in.

Audrey grabs my hand and leads me along the corridor and down a small flight of stairs. I bet she could find her way there blindfold if she had to.

"Who was that?" I whisper to her.

"The night porter," she says. "Petheridge."

No wonder there was no sign of anybody when we blundered into the broom cupboard. Petheridge obviously confines his activities to the upper floors.

"He doesn't share, does he?" I ask nervously.

As I have said before, I am not a great one for unveiling my nasty in the presence of others than those who have been invited to witness the experience.

"Not on Thursdays," she says comfortingly and pushes the door open on a small room smelling of Boots After Shave lotion. There, to my relief, is a tiny cot, empty as the day it left the great bed maker. I do not wait to look under it for burglars but pull Audrey to me and slip my hands under her skirt as if picking a mushroom. Her tongue nearly beats mine to the draw and we fondle each other like a couple of kids with their first wad of plasticine. Normally, on such occasions, I expect to play some part in removing my partner's clothes, but this chick is such an enthusiast that she is pulling down her tights before I have unzipped a boot. In less time than it takes to sign for a registered envelope from ERNIE she is lying back on the bed with only a small heart-shaped necklet in danger of being crushed out of shape between her boobs.

"You look lovely," I tell her.

"Shut up with all that flannel," she says. "I'm not putting up a fight."

She is right, of course. It is just that I am so used to saying it that it has become a habit with me.

I strip down to my pink candy-striped underpants—everybody is wearing them in Clapham this year—and climb on to the bed. It is not that I am modest. Just that I don't see why the bird should not do a little work for it. Her greedy little hand slides down over my belly and I close in on her mouth. She has the most fantastic skin. Like a slightly bruised peach. I slide one hand beneath her shoulders and send the other down to do a recce for J.T. Everything seems more than ready so with a quick nibble around the bits that give baby his elevenses, I climb aboard and we motor round the bay a couple of times. She is quite a girl, this Audrey. Very strong in the pelvis and capable of opening Tizer bottles with her belly button I should reckon. I can see why Petheridge hangs around her bedroom. It must be better than sorting out the early calls. I am trying to control myself but with this girl thudding away underneath you it is like trying to put out a forest fire with a can of petrol. She suddenly starts groaning hoarsely and then squealing so loud that everyone in the hotel must be able to hear her. Nothing turns me on faster than a woman's moans and in no time at all I am ebbing away between her thighs, beautifully taken out of myself.

"I can hear your heart beating," she murmurs.

"Thank God," I say. "I was worried there, for a minute."

Maybe I am getting old or perhaps it is just that I have had a busy day. Anyway, I immediately begin to feel sleepy and climb gratefully between the sheets as Audrey looks about her wistfully.

"I think I'll go and see if that man is still sleeping in our room," she says. "I won't be a minute."

I mumble something and close my eyes as I listen to the

45

sea hissing against the shingle—we don't have much sand on our part of the beach. There is a shaded lamp on the table beside the bed and this bathes the room in a soft, warm glow. Lucky Timmy. The door opens and I hear Audrey come in. I do not change my position but nuzzle deeper into the pillow and make "I am almost asleep, please do not disturb" noises. I will catch up with her again in the morning, Petheridge willing.

Strange that I can hear the delicious sound of nylon being peeled away from flesh. Why should Audrey have put on her tights to go up one flight of stairs? I turn my head to take a quick butchers and—blimey oh Riley! There, bending forward to shed her bra is the receptionist bird Sandra. The one I took an instant fancy to. She must have an understanding with Petheridge as well. No wonder the bloke sleeps so much!

Without looking towards the bed she slips out of her panties, gives a delicious little shiver that makes her tits wobble invitingly and pulls back the sheets. It is in this far-from-unattractive pose that our eyes meet for the first time that evening.

"Oh." she says. "I wasn't expecting to see you."

"Me neither."

"What are you doing here?"

"Come inside and we'll talk about it."

She gives a little shrug and begins to climb into the bed.

"Oh well," she says. "Life's so short, isn't it?"

CHAPTER THREE

"Quite like old times, it was," says Sid wolfing down half a kipper in one mouthful. "Good to know that the old unquenchable magnetism is still coming on like the Chinese cavalry."

"Very reassuring, Sid," I say, trying to keep my eyes open. By the cringe, but that Sandra is a goer. Maybe it is something to do with the sea air. I reckon someone like

46

her must have had a go at Nelson. He lost his eye and his arm and then he said "Right! That's it!" and hopped up on his column. Female spiders are supposed to nosh up their mates after having it away, aren't they?

"I didn't tell you what happened, did I?" continues Sid who is clearly going to.

"It was amazing, really. I've been in some funny situations in my time, but—hey, wake up! Your rice krispies are going all soggy. What's the matter with you?—anyway, where was I? Oh yes, I'd just finished driving her into a fit of uncontrollable ecstasy for about the seventeenth time when suddenly the door opens and in pops your one. Before I can say 'half-time, change ends', she's hopped into bed with us! How about that then? I have to admire her taste but, blimey! It's brazen, isn't it? Doesn't say much for your performance either—stop yawning!"

"Sorry, Sid. I did have a few problems myself last night."

"Sounds like it." Sid is obviously dead chuffed with himself and in such moods is considerably less than lovable.

"Yeah, that receptionist bird Sandra nobbled me—nibbled me a bit as well."

"What!" Sid's toast quivers outside his mush.

"Some kind of strange magnetism I exude must have drawn her to me. It was funny, really, just like you say. I had just finished driving my bird into a fit of uncontrollable ecstasy for—oh, I suppose it must have been about the twenty-fifth time—when Sandra springs through the door like a female tigress—"

"As opposed to a male tigress," says Sid.

"Precisely. 'Leave him,' she cries, 'that man is mine,' and she picks up Audrey and chucks her through the door like she is a sack of feathers. After that, well I don't really know how to describe it. She just tears the bedclothes off and has her ruthless way with me until cockcrow—or in my case, cockcroak."

"Go on! You're kidding."

"Straight up, Sid—or at least it was to start with."

"I don't believe you."

"Please yourself."

47

At that moment Sandra comes into the dining room throwing out more curves than a Scalextric track.

"Hello tiger," she says raping me with a warm smile as she goes past our table.

"More toast, Sidney?" I say politely.

Half an hour later we are outside leaning against the sea wall and admiring the patterns the oil slicks make on the water.

"One thing I don't understand, Sid," I say. "Who is supposed to be running this place at the moment?"

"A woman called Miss Ruperts. She used to own it once and then sold out to Funfrall. She's an alcoholic apparently. Goes off to be dried out occasionally."

"I can imagine this place driving you to drink. Blimey, what with her and Mrs. Caitley, it's going to be a nice little set-up, isn't it? Does Miss Ruperts know you're taking over?"

"She should have heard this morning. Sir Giles wrote to her at the sanatorium."

"So she's away on a cure at the moment?"

"Yeah. She should be in peak form at the moment."

As he says the words, an ancient Armstrong Siddeley can be seen belting down the promenade towards us. Its course is, to put it mildly, erratic, and it forces a milk float off the road before squealing to a halt outside the Cromby. Hardly have the wheels stopped turning than the driver's door flies open and a big woman of about fifty gets out. She is carrying a bulging suitcase and has only taken two steps before the case bursts open and about half a dozen spirit bottles shatter on the paving stones.

"What did you say her name was?" I ask Sid.

"Miss Ruperts," he says grimly.

" 'In peak form', that's what you said, isn't it Sid? Looks as if she's heard the news all right."

"Shut up," says Sid.

"I expect you want to go and introduce yourself. I think I'll take a turn round the pier."

I watch Miss R. lurch through the front entrance of the hotel.

48

"You come with me," hisses Sid. "You're my Personal Assistant. This is what you get paid for."

"When, Sid?" I ask, but he does not seem to hear me. I follow him across the road and we bump into Miss Primstone just outside the hotel.

"Was—er—that Miss Ruperts?" says Sidney casually.

"Yes," says Miss Primstone hurriedly. "But she seems rather overtired. I think she wants to be alone."

"Very understandable," says Sid. "But could you tell her that Mr. Noggett would like a word with her? It is important."

"Have you ever thought about changing your name?" I say as Miss P. hurries away shaking her head.

"Shut up."

"But Sidney Noggett. I mean, it's not like Gaylord Mandeville, is it?"

"No, thank God. Now belt up! Unless you want to start sketching the insides of Labour Exchanges for a living."

"That's very funny, Sid," I say as we are shown into a small dark office behind the reception. "Have you ever thought about doing it professionally?"

"I've thought about doing you, hundreds of times. Ah, Miss Ruperts? How nice to have the pleasure of making your acquaintance. I am Sidney Noggett and this is my Personal Assistant Mr. Lea."

"A bauble," says Miss R. as she pours a jumbo shot of Scotch into a shaking tumbler.

"I beg your pardon?"

"To be a bauble passed from hand to hand is not the future I would have envisaged for myself in those halcyon days of yore." I don't really understand what she is on about because I have edited out the slurs so it reads understandably. But "passed from hand to hand"? With her frame you would need a fork lift truck. She has a mug like a professional wrestler—only most of them shave these days— and hair like Wild Bill Hitchcock—feminine but masculine, if you know what I mean. Her shoulders would not be out of place on a second row forward. And, how often does Raquel Welch wear a Norfolk jacket and jodhpurs with a

49

bootlace tie? You can count the times on the notches of your riding crop. All in all, a very distinctive lady, not much prone to flower arrangement, or anything else, I would wager.

"Have no fear, madam," says Sidney who picked up most of his manners from old movies starring the likes of Ronald Coleman. "You have no cause for alarm."

"Casting an eye over the register used to be like glancing through Debrett. Half the crowned heads of Europe stayed here. Their servants used to put up at the Grand. And now, now—" Miss Ruperts chokes with emotion, or maybe it is the booze. "I am on my way to the gutter." She knocks back the contents of her glass and belches loudly. Now you would not think that D.D.T. "No flies on me" Noggett would be taken in by that load of cobblers, would you? No? Well, you would be wrong. Very wrong. Sidney—and I am not so different myself, really—has a respect for anything uppercrust that is positively terrifying. If some bloke had rolled up flashing his greasy braces and with half a Woodbine glued to his lower lip, Sidney would have taken him apart soon as look at him, but this drunken old slagbag is getting the Queen Mother treatment because she talks very refained and does not remind Sid of anything he has seen in Scraggs Lane—ancestral home of the Leas.

"Miss Ruperts, allow me to assure you—"

But Miss R. has not finished yet.

"It is not me that I am thinking of," she says, reaching out for the Scotch bottle, "but those faithful retainers who have rendered yeoman service all these years. Treat me as you will, I have my memories to live on, but I beseech you, do not cast them into the wilderness. This place has been a home to them. To you it may only be a realisable asset but—please! I beseech you. Temper expediency with mercy."

You don't read speeches like that in Shakespeare, do you? Certainly not if it's a choice between that and Coronation Street.

"Miss Ruperts," says Sid, while I wonder if I am hearing right. "I am certain that your experience will be invaluable.

50

I hope that we will be able to work together to restore the hotel to its former position of immenseness. Do not fear that I have any plans to destroy your life work."

Miss Ruperts is visibly moved by these stirring words and has to take more liquid comfort to calm herself.

"Call me a stupid old woman if you will," she begins.

"You're a—"

"Shut up, Timmy! Forgive me, Miss Ruperts. You were saying."

"Nothing. Nothing at all. I was only attempting an expression of gratitude for your noble gesture and generous sentiments. Now, if you will forgive me, I would like to be left alone. The events of the last few hours have taken toll of my strength—my heart, you know. She taps the region of her enormous chest which looks like a kitbag worn on the wrong side of the body.

"Of course, of course," Sid is backing out of the office. "We can discuss details later. I hope you will soon be perfectly recovered."

"I hope you know what you're doing," I say as we return to the cocktail bar. "You weren't really swallowing all that rubbish were you?"

"One of the old school," says Sid. "You don't often meet them like that these days."

"If you're lucky you don't. Come off it, Sid. She's a piss artist. If you don't get rid of her, she'll drink the place dry within a couple of weeks."

"She does have a drink problem, I'll grant you that, but she must be worth a lot of goodwill in a place like this. Think of the contacts she's got."

"I'd rather not, though I suppose she might be able to fix us up with an Alcoholics Anonymous Convention. I thought you were going to weed out all the layabouts? She'd be top of my list."

"I'll be the judge of that, and make sure you don't start creeping up the charts. If we can keep her under control, I'm certain she can do us some good. I don't want to start off with any unpleasantness."

"It's because she's got a posh voice, that's what it is.

You're just like dad when there's a whiff of the nobility about."

I can see that Sid is getting the needle and this impression is confirmed by his next remarks.

"Let's forget about Miss Ruperts for a minute," he says, "and let's talk about what you're going to do."

"Your Personal Assistant," I say brightly.

"That kind of thing," Sid nods his head slowly. "But first of all you've got to learn the ropes. I've already mentioned that this place needs a commissionaire."

"You don't expect me to hang about outside all day in some poncy uniform, do you?"

"Not all day, Timmy, no. You are going to have so many other things to do, there won't be time—waiting, working in the kitchens, portering—"

"Hey, wait a minute!"

"No 'heys', Timothy. I want you to undertake a thorough apprenticeship in the hotel business. I only wish I could join you myself."

"Why can't you?"

"Lazy majesty. It's a French expression meaning that if you are the boss you are expected to ponce about all day doing nothing, otherwise it upsets people."

"It wouldn't upset me, Sid."

"You are not people, Timmo."

"But they're going to think I'm some kind of nark, Sid."

"Of course they won't. They won't realise you are reporting back everything you hear to me, unless you choose to tell them. This experience is going to be vital, Timmy, because you'll be able to learn about every fiddle the staff are pulling, from the inside."

"I don't like it, Sid."

"Well, you know what you can do then. What did you think you would be doing? Sitting in a little office in a pinstripe suit?"

"It would make a change from some of the things I've been doing lately."

But, of course, Sid has me firmly under his thumb and when I appear at the meeting at which he addresses the staff,

I don't even get a place on the platform. Miss Ruperts introduces him and it would make you sick to hear the way she goes on. She must have sworn off the stuff for a couple of hours beforehand because her hands are not shaking and every word comes over crystal clear. "Better days ahead", "Exciting new prospects", "Marching forward into the seventies", are some of the golden oldies that come tripping off her tongue and these are only bettered by Sid who bounds to his feet and gives his all in true Funfrall manner. I am quite pleased to find that nobody registers any enthusiasm at all except Mrs. Caitley who says "Hear! hear!" periodically through Miss Ruperts' address. I later learn that they were land girls together during the war and have been in tandem ever since. What a diabolical thought! Milk production must have dropped off something awful when the cows saw those two flexing their pinkies.

Sid eventually draws to a close, one of the hall porters farts and there is a ripple of applause. I personally think it is for the fart, which is quite an effective one. What is interesting is to observe the reaction of Sandra, June and Audrey now that they know who we are. The last two seem to think that they have been conned while Sandra is clearly impressed. All through Sid's speech she gazes at him like he has just discovered how to make gold bars from fag ends and her contribution is a sizeable slice of the ripple of applause that greets the end of his ramble through cliché land.

On the other hand, she looks through me like an empty goldfish bowl and I feel it is going to be some time before I get another piece of nooky from that quarter. The fact that I am posted to the kitchens on the first part of my training course does not help matters. In my greasy clobber I hardly look likely to give Smoothiechops a run for his money.

Make no mistake about it. The people who work in the kitchens of large hotels are not likely to crop up in the Vogue social column very often. Some of them are rough. Very rough. If it was not for the frying pans I would have thought I was in the engine room of an Albanian minesweeper lent to the Irish navy. One bloke is tattooed from

53

head to toe and keeps gulping down swigs of meths whilst there are two Spaniards who cannot understand a word of English and spend most of the time holding hands behind the chip slicer.

The female presence, apart from Mrs. Caitley, is virtually non-existent and I, for one, am grateful. When you look around you it is easy to see why chefs are usually men—big, strong men. It is a tribute to Mrs. Caitley's muscle power that she can wield any authority at all and still have enough strength left for her marathon hassle with Mr. "Superpouf" Bentley—that is the name of the maitre d'hotel, or head waiter to you and me. Normally, the chef de cuisine has total authority over the choice and preparation of meals and Mr. B. is pushing his luck in trying to get in on the act.

That is another thing you soon learn when you work in a hotel. Everybody is "Mr. This" and "Mr. That". There is none of the informality that used to prevail at the holiday camp. This is presumably because everybody in the business seems to have worked their way up from the bottom and is very jealous of preserving their status.

And talking of working your way up from the bottom, I have never seen so many concrete parachutes in my life. I have nothing against queers, except the toe of my boot if they become too persistent, but really! After peeling millions of potatoes and scraping blackened cooking pots in a temperature of over a hundred degrees, and in an atmosphere so steamy that you can hardly see the dripping walls, the last thing you fancy is being touched up by some joker as you bend over to sluice your greens.

My dismissal to the kitchen does at least help my relationship with June and Audrey. Like everyone else on the staff, they trust me less than a Vietnamese threepenny bit but at least when they see me crawling along the corridors towards my new room—yes, Sid has moved into the management suite and I have been relegated to the "Penthouse Club" or attic, as it is also known—they realise that being a nark is not all easy sailing.

"Trying a bit of work for a change are you?" says June

as we bump into each other on my first evening.

"Don't be like that. I'm knackered."

She is all tarted up and obviously about to grab a bit of the gay night life that Hoverton has to offer before it closes down at half past nine.

"Why aren't you downstairs with your mate?"

"You ask him that. He wants me to learn the ropes. At the moment I feel like hanging myself with one of them."

"It's not nice down there, is it?" says June with a hint of sympathy creeping into her voice. "You have to be careful when you come out into the cold. It's easy to catch a chill."

"I'll remember that. Where are you going?"

"They have a dance down at the Pier on Fridays. Do you fancy coming?"

"I'm not much of a dancer at the best of times and tonight I couldn't stand up for the national anthem. Thanks anyway. Another time."

"You sure you're all right?"

"Oh yes. Just fagged out, that's all."

I let myself into my room and notice her registering its number.

"I'll see you later," she says. "Bring you a little surprise. Who are you sharing with?"

"Nobody at the moment. I think the bloke is on holiday or evaporated."

"Oh." Her face lights up. "See you."

She trips off down the corridor and I peel off my clobber, have a sluice down in the washbasin and climb on to the bed to listen to the plumbing. It is just like being back at home with the sloping rafters inches from my nose.

I must have drifted off because the next thing I am aware of is a burst of laughter in the corridor and the sound of whispering and giggling right outside my door. I open my eyes as the door knob turns and June and Audrey come in wearing long nightdresses with frills at neck and hem. Very nice too. What is an additional peeper-bonus is the playmate they have brought with them. A coloured girl I have been quietly eyeing since I crossed the threshold. She is

55

wearing a black shortie nightdress and carrying a bottle of brown ale.

"Have you got an opener?" she says and all three of them burst into fits of giggles.

"You had a good evening, did you?" I say, waking up fast and slipping my hand under the sheets to adjust periscope.

"We brought you a present," says the coloured chick.

"Which one?" I say, looking from one to the other of them. More giggles.

"This is Carmen," says Audrey. "She said she'd like to meet you."

"I never did."

"You did."

"I never."

I imagine that Carmen is blushing but it is difficult to tell.

"Anyhow," I say gallantly to cover her embarrassment, "the brown ale is for me, is it?"

"Yes. We thought you needed building up." More giggles. If the sheets were transparent, they might change their minds.

"I'll have to open it, won't I? Look the other way, girls."

I grab a handy towel and drape it around my shapely loins as I slide out of bed. I don't have an opener but I reckon I can knock the top off on the edge of the table— that and a few other things.

"Hold this penny, luv."

Carmen leans forward and I get an eyeful of lovely dusky knocker. Colour problem? You must be joking! It would be no problem for me, I can tell you. I hook the bottle top over the edge of the coin and give it a hard bash with my fist. Hard enough, anyway, to drive it down on to my bare toe. I scream loudly and drop the towel whereupon it is the girls' turn to scream loudly. I don't know what they are making all the fuss about. They have probably seen better and they must have seen worse.

"Press down on the coin this time. O.K., luv?"

Carmen nods and her face is a study in concentration as the mighty Lea fist is raised again. This time I give it a

56

right belt and the top flies off—no trouble. Unfortunately it has become resentful of the treatment dished out to it and promptly discharges its contents over Carmen's shorty night-dress. The poor bird is soaked to her lovely skin and when the flimsy material sticks to her it becomes transparent. No wonder that in all the excitement my towel falls off again. Hey ho, some things were clearly meant to be, eh? I slip my arm around Carmen's waist and raise one and a half inches of brown froth to my lips.

"Cheers, girls, thanks a lot. That was a very nice gesture. Now, what can I do for you?"

A diabolically stupid question you may well say, but I am a great one for observing the niceties. A tidal wave of female flesh bears me back on to the bed which promptly collapses under the strain. I don't know what these birds have been drinking but it sure beats the hell out of diluted yogurt. None of them are slow starters but this jungle bunny Carmen climbs over me like I am a commando training course closely followed by the other two in flying T formation. I am fighting for sexual survival as I try to work out what I should be doing to which. In the end I give up and have a stab at anything that is moving. And, dear readers, there is a lot moving. Luckily my experiences with Nat and Nan have taught me the basic rudiments—and I do mean rude-iments! If there was going to be an action replay you would need about fourteen cameras to capture all the detail. And the noise. Oh, my God, the noise! That must be what attracts Miss Primstone. I get my head up just in time to see her turning in to a great black prune in the doorway.

"Urgh!" she says. "Urgh!" The noise is rather like a dog growling through a bone it is worrying. "I am going to re-port this disgusting behaviour to the management."

She is just like the two old bags on the train because she shows no sign of going away but stands there drinking in the monstrous depravity and loving every moment.

"I'm going to get on top of him now," says Carmen. "Do you want to watch that?"

Only then does the door close and Carmen makes good her threat—or promise, depending on which way you look at it. It is all good, clean, healthy fun in the modern tradition but I don't think that Miss Primstone has nipped off to tell her diary about it. As Carmen gently rises and falls across my hips I can imagine the tales that are now being borne along the corridors of power. Reinforcements will soon be on their way.

"Girls, girls!" I bleat pathetically. "Don't you think we'd better stop? We'll all get the sack."

"I'd like to see them try. We can do what we like in our spare time."

"'Spare' is right," I wheeze. "Now, get off me before something terrible happens."

But it is like King Canute telling the waves to put a sock in it. The girls come at me as if they are trying to find pieces to keep as souvenirs. I struggle gamely, of course, but ten hours in the Cromby kitchen takes a lot out of you. It is becoming more like careless rupture than rapture.

Just when I can take no more, and give even less, the door flies open, and there, wearing curlers and a nightdress that looks like a dust sheet borrowed from a grand piano, is Miss Ruperts. She is carrying a shooting stick and this she promptly applies to June's shapely rear portions.

"Out, hussies! Out!!" she barks. "Disgusting little animals. Back to your lair, Jezebel." With that remark, Carmen cops a sharp prod on the sit-me-down. Miss Ruperts is obviously a very rustic lady and she lashes out with her shooting stick like she is making hay with it. In no time at all the birds have grabbed their nighties and scuttled out into the corridor and I am left to bear the full brunt of Miss Ruperts' wrath.

"And what have you got to say for yourself, you mongrel?" she scolds. The shooting stick is hovering dangerously near my Action Man Kit and for a moment I have a nasty feeling that Miss R. may be contemplating doing a park keeper with it.

"I didn't invite them," I whine. "I was trying to sleep."

"You're Mr. Noggett's protégé, aren't you?" she says suddenly, peering down at me. "I wonder what he'll have to say about this."

"I don't know. I should think—"

"Put your pyjamas on and we will find out."

"What! Hey, wait a minute. We don't want to disturb him now, surely. The whole thing was a joke that got out of hand. We weren't really doing anything."

"Come," Miss R. waves her shooting stick as if she means business.

"But—"

"Get up! Don't try and hide your pathetic body. I've mated horses."

There seems to be nothing for it but to do as she says. So I pull on my pyjama bottoms and give her my pleading look. It does no good.

"Come on. We will go and see Mr. Noggett."

Sidney is not going to like this, I think to myself as I am marched down the corridor sandwiched between Miss Ruperts and Miss Primstone. Now he has become Conrad Hilton he has rediscovered many of the little ways that made him such a prize tit when he was with Funfrall.

Knock, knock! Miss R. turns the handle before the sound has died away and I stumble into Sidney's suite. Very nice, very nice indeed. Large settees, candelabra, a tray of drinks —Sandra is looking nice, too. She pops up from the sofa as the door flies open. Too bad she appears to be naked. Sidney, too, as we see when his red face and ruffled hair appear a couple of seconds later.

"Sorry to trouble you, Sid," I say evenly. "But Miss Ruperts wants a word with you."

"Oh."

I say "oh" because I turn round to find that Miss Ruperts and Miss Primstone are leaving the room like it might start sinking at any moment. I guess that is the end of them for the evening.

"Carry on, Sid," I say. "I expect she'll take it up with you in the morning."

I leave the room quickly, before he can throw anything at me.

CHAPTER FOUR

Sidney is very upset the next morning, when he calls me into his office, and it takes a long time before I can make him believe that coming round to his room was not my idea.

"She said I was your protégé," I tell him.

"Dirty old faggot. She should mind what she says," explodes Sid. "You can end up in court saying things like that. I've never fancied a fellow in my life."

"She probably realised that when she saw you with Sandra," I comfort him.

"Yeah. What were you up to, then?"

I tell him about June, Audrey and Carmen and I can see his face cloud over immediately. Sort of a green cloud, it is.

"You want to watch out," he says finally. "Two last night. Three tonight. Where's it all going to end? How long before you're dragging your mattress down to the tele lounge?"

"Give over, Sid. Most of them are old enough to be my grandmother. And what about you, anyway?"

"I'm cutting back. Only one last night. Anyway, it's different in my case. In my position its practically staff relations."

"Any truth in the rumour that you've got Miss Ruperts lined up for tonight?"

Sid shudders. "Do me a favour, I've never fancied myself in jodhpurs. Still, I'd better do something to sweeten her up, hadn't I?"

"Why bother? Give her the riding boot, Sid."

"No, I can't do that. I still think she could be useful."

"You're barmy, Sid."

"Watch it, Timothy—"

Whenever he calls me Timothy, I know he is rattled.

"—remember who's in charge. About time you were down in the kitchen, isn't it?"

"How much longer do I have to stay there, Sid? The heat is sapping my strength."

"Not enough, by all accounts. You give it another two days, and we'll see if you're nearly ready for waiter service."

"But, Sid—"

"No buts. Now push off. I've got to see Miss Ruperts."

So I go down to the basement to find that one of the sous chefs has resigned and the Chef Tournant—he turns his hand to anything, see?—gone to hospital. The two occurrences are not unconnected because the Sous Chef has resigned by pouring a pot of coffee down the front of the Chef Tournant's baggy trousers. Very nasty! Passions do run high in the kitchens and with the heat and the foreigners you feel you are working in the middle of a jungle clearing sometimes. Only "She Who Must Be Obeyed" holds us all together.

For some strange reason Mrs. Caitley seems to take a fancy to me and gives me a friendly bash on the shoulder once we have provided the Chef Tournant with half a pound of lard to slide down the front of his pants.

"I hear you were a naughty boy last night," she says gruffly. "Take my advice. Don't get mixed up with any of the fillies in this place. Rotten little scrubbers most of them. Find yourself reporting to the vet in no time."

She is putting it a bit strongly but there is no doubt that the staff in the Cromby—both male and female—have considerably more sex-drive than your grandma's tabby. To wander about the upper floor of the hotel after ten o'clock at night you need to be fitted with bumpers. Luckily my room mate comes back from holiday and he is so repulsive that not even the randiest bird in the place wants to get through the door.

It is not until I progress from the kitchens to becoming a waiter that I have what you might call my first brush with one of the paying customers. To be exact, I become a commis waiter. This is the humblest form of life in the dining room and is the bloke who brings the grub from the kitchen and puts it down on the table for the chef du rang to slap down in front of the customers. After a few days of doing this you may be allowed to serve a portion of vegetables as a special treat. A Chef du Rang is a senior waiter who looks after a few tables, and aspires to eventually become a maitre d'hotel. Fascinating, isn't it? No? Oh, well, please yourself.

One morning, as I go into the dining room, I get an elbow in the ribs from Petheridge the night porter, who is just going to turn in after his labours. He, you may remember, is the gentleman who was spread out starkers on Audrey's bed and is no stranger to a spot of the other.

"Couple of right little love birds flew in last night," he says with a leer. "Table Six."

"They up already?"

"About half a dozen times, I should reckon." He gives me another nudge. "No. I expect they couldn't sleep for the excitement. Hey, that Carmen's a one, isn't she? I've heard of Carmen Rollers, but she's ridiculous. Damn near broke up my set."

Petheridge is a big, strapping bloke with a jaw line that makes Charlton Heston look like a nancy boy. The thought of him and Carmen on the job is enough to keep the blue movie industry in ideas for years.

"Yes," I say. "Very nice. Sleep tight, Peth."

He ambles off scratching the front of his trousers and I go into the dining room. Table Six. Oh yes! At first I can hardly see them because they are so small but there sit this teeny couple with honeymoon written all over them. The bloke is wearing his short-sleeved multi-patterned holiday shirt with matching scarf and has a camera on the table in front of him so he can rush out and start snapping everything that moves and the girl is all scrubbed and virginal with her hair pulled back from her face and her skin glowing with health and expectation. She blushes like fury when the bloke asks her whether she would prefer tea or coffee and goes berserk pouring it out for him. Not like the other married couples in the room who just stretch out their hands for pieces of toast from behind spread newspapers.

"Do you know what the weather forecast is?" says the

bird brightly when I bring them some more marmalade. The bloke loves his marmalade.

"I think they said we were in for a fine spell."

"Oh, goody. Did you hear that, Roger? Lots of lovely pickies."

She turns to me. "My, my—husband is very keen on photography."

"Not very good, though," says hubby bashfully.

"Oh, darling! You've won the club trophy two years running. And what about that photograph you had published in Camera News. 'The Old Forge by Moonlight'."

"It was very dark."

"That was the way they printed it, darling."

She turns to me again. "Don't you listen to him. He's awfully good, really."

What a nice kid! I think to myself. Ain't love grand? Nice to know that there are still a few pleasant, uncomplicated people about. I avoid Carmen's glance as she sneaks into the dining room. One thing you can never tell about her is whether she has dark rings under her eyes.

In the days that follow, I begin to take a special interest in love's young dream and it is therefore a surprise when, one morning, only Roger appears at the breakfast table. He is looking strained—a condition which does not totally surprise me—and fiddling uneasily with the cord of his Leica.

"Shall I wait for modom?" I say thoughtfully.

"No. She's having breakfast in her room today. Just a cup of coffee for me, thanks."

A cup of coffee? That is hardly the stuff to give Wee Georgie Wood the strength to blow up a couple of balloons for a kid's birthday party. What ails our boy? Whilst others nosh back their sausage and egg, Roger gazes glumly out of the windows towards the oil tankers which are leaking slowly across the horizon. When he eventually departs, his coffee is cold and untouched and there is no sign of wifey. I watch carefully and he does not go upstairs but leaves the hotel and walks slowly along the promenade. He is not heading for civilisation, but open country. For the first time that

I can remember he has not taken a picture of anything before he disappears from sight.

What is up? A lover's tiff? I wonder what wifey's mood is at this moment. To find out I ask the waiter who has taken her breakfast up. Tear-stained and without appetite, are his comments and he has an untouched tray to prove it. Mrs. Richards does not come down until eleven o'clock and sits by herself writing postcards until lunch time when Mr. R. returns and they go silently in to lunch. After lunch they go up to their room and then it is Mrs. R. who emerges, her eyes wet with tears, and goes off by herself.

The next day they are down to breakfast together but there is an air of crushing silence about them that makes me clear my throat every time I decide to speak. They spend the day together but in the evening it is Mr. Richards who eats alone in the dining room while his wife takes her meal upstairs.

On the third day I become elevated to floor service and see neither of them but the fourth I am told that there is a breakfast to be taken up to Number Six. One breakfast! I tap discreetly on the door and a voice so low I can hardly hear it tells me to come in. Mrs. Richards is propped up on a couple of pillows and, as far as I can see, is alone. Again, she looks red-eyed with crying.

"Are you going to have it in bed, modom?"

She looks at me for a long moment and then her lower lip starts trembling.

"Now come on," I say. "Don't—"

But it is no good. She bursts into floods of tears and throws herself face down on the bed.

"I'm sorry, I'm sorry," she moans.

"Come on, cheer up," I say. "Look, I've brought you a nice kipper."

I feel a right berk saying that, but what can you do in the circumstances? "Shall I fetch the doctor; I think he's sobered up—I mean up and about." Stupid slip, that, but like everyone else in the place, Dr. McDonald seems partial to his "wee drappy".

64

"No. I don't need a doctor. No, I'm sorry. Leave the tray. I'll see if I can face something later."

"Shall I find your husband?"

At the mention of the word "husband" she starts sobbing twice as violently and buries her face in the pillow. I try and comfort her but she waves me away and in the end I find myself shaking my head in the corridor.

I see neither her nor her husband for the rest of that day and imagine that they must have checked out. It is therefore a surprise when, next morning, I am told to take breakfast to Room Six. Again, just one breakfast.

This time there is a more cheerful response to my knock on the door and I notice that Mrs. Richards is wearing a frilly nightdress and a trace of make-up.

"Morning," she says brightly, before I can open my mouth. The sparkle in her eyes may be the remnant of a tear or a return to the mood she was in when I first saw her.

"Morning."

"I'm sorry about yesterday. I was very down in the dumps. I don't know what came over me." While she is talking her hands are gripping the edge of the counterpane and she looks into my eyes as if trying to find something.

"Don't worry. I expect you felt a bit strange, being married and all that." I know Peter O'Toole would have put it better, but he had the education.

"You're very understanding. Do you often get women who burst into tears all over you?"

"Not so far. I've only been doing this job for a week."

I give her a quick rundown on my curriculum vitae—no madam, it does not mean what you think it does—and she nods understandingly.

"So you're new at it, too?"

I am not quite certain what she means, so I give her a sympathetic smile—at least, I hope it is sympathetic—and keep my mouth shut.

"I've brought you some nice grapefruit segments," I say eventually, as her eyes continue to follow the passage of the blood round my body.

"You're so kind, you always try and bring me something nice, don't you?"

"It's all part of the service."

She is a very appealing bird, this one, and I can feel myself getting my guinea-pig stroking syndrome (I got that word from "It Pays to Increase Your Word Power". Thank you, Reader's Digest.)

"Roger said you were kind." Her lip starts to tremble. Oh, no ! I can't stand this again.

"Shall I open the windows?" I say hurriedly. "It's a lovely day again."

"It's all right. I'm not going to cry. I'm sorry." She puts down the bedclothes and smiles up at me. "Are you married?"

"Blimey no. I mean, I've nothing against marriage of course. It's just that I don't think I'm ready for it."

"I should think you're more married than I am." I don't know what she means and my expression telegraphs it. "I'm sorry," she continues, "I wasn't trying to be abstruse."

Just as well, I think, because I dont know what it means.

"I mean," and then she pauses.

"Yes?" I say helpfully.

"My marriage hasn't worked out quite the way I thought it would."

"Oh well, it's early days yet. I've heard it takes a little getting used to. They say the first ten years are the worst." Her lip starts to tremble again. "I was only joking, of course."

"Sex." The word comes out of her mouth like a bullet.

"Would you like it on your lap?" I swallow hard. "I mean, the tray, of course."

"I haven't. We've not—"

"I'll pour you some coffee, shall I?"

"He's always taking photographs."

"I've noticed. Careful, you're spilling your grapefruit."

"He said he respected me."

"That's very nice."

"I've never—"

"That's not so unusual. I mean—"

66

"Neither has he."

"Oh."

The juice from her grapefruit segments has leaked on to the toast and she is looking out of the window as she talks as if speaking into a tape recorder.

"I'd better take that before you spill everything."

"Oh, sorry. I don't really feel hungry anyway."

"Where is he now?"

"Roger?"

"Yes."

"It sounds stupid but I think he's gone home to mother."

"He's left you?"

"Not permanently. No, he was upset. We were both upset. I am upset. He's coming back, I think. Oh, I don't know." She looks as if she is about to burst into tears again.

"Because you can't—er—I mean, because you—er—haven't got it together yet?"

"'Is there something wrong with us?' I've read books about it. Every magazine you pick up is full of articles about it." She suddenly looks me straight in the eyes. "I'm sorry. You must think I'm mad talking to you like this."

"No, no. That's fine. It must be very trying for you."

"I feel that if I don't tell somebody about it, I'll go mad. I can't talk to my mother. She wouldn't understand and it would make her unhappy."

"You've talked to your husband about it?"

"I've tried to, but you see, it's difficult, because—he can't, he hasn't been able to." She blushes furiously.

"It's probably nerves," I say. "There have been times when I was all tensed up and I couldn't—er—you know—"

"Get it together?" She manages a smile.

"That's right."

"But—forgive me asking this. You can tell me to mind my own business if you like—the first time you made love, was it so difficult? I'm assuming that you're not a virgin."

"No, I'm not," I say looking at the ceiling. "Well, let me see. It was a bit different for me because the bird I was—I mean, the lady in question was what you might call experienced." You might also have called her a raving nympho

67

but I don't want to labour the point. I can still remember us writhing amongst the potato peelings, the rain bashing down outside the kitchen window, my squeegee propped against the broom cupboard—happy days! "I don't imagine," I go on, "that you have ever? No, of course, you said you hadn't. And probably not, how shall I put it, fiddled about much either?"

"My hymen has never been ruptured."

"I'm very glad to hear it," I say. I mean, it does sound nasty, doesn't it? My Uncle Harry had a lot of trouble when his—"What I'm trying to say is that I am still a complete virgin," says the bird.

"Oh. Yes. Well that can be a problem. I don't think I've ever—er—had the pleasure with a virgin, if you know what I mean."

"Never?"

"No, not never. Your husband is one, too, isn't he?"

"Yes."

"Very ticklish. Like you say. You get the idea there aren't many around these days. I know that's wrong, of course. I've read those surveys in the Sundays. Most girls are still virgins when they get married, aren't they? It must be the circles I move in, I suppose."

"So you can't help me?" Her face goes even redder. "I mean, with advice."

"Not speaking from experience, no."

Suddenly, I get an idea which would have occurred to any sane bloke about ten minutes before. I sit down on the bed and put my foot in her saucer of marmalade. That was not the idea, I hasten to add. Just a typical bit of Lea misfortune. I push the tray under the bed with my heel and rub the gunge off against the side of the bedside table.

"I would like to help you, though," I say. "I don't think it would be very difficult, really I don't."

I look into her soft, brown eyes and she turns her head away.

"If you mean what I think you mean, I couldn't. It would be adultery. I couldn't commit adultery on my honeymoon."

"Don't look at it like that," I say hurriedly. "What I'm suggesting is a step towards a complete marriage. That's what you want, isn't it?"

"Yes, but it seems so underhand."

"There's nothing underhand about it. You'd be doing it for him, really."

The more I think about it, the more I am convincing myself that it is a marvellous idea. She is a very cute little chick and there is only one of her. Sidney is right. I am getting a bit brassed off with all this group activity. Also, I would be performing a public service—in a manner of speaking. That's always a nice way to wrap up a bit of in and out.

"But me being a virgin. That's not all the trouble. He doesn't seem to be able to—"

"First things first," I say comfortingly. "Let's get you sorted out then we can think about him. I'm certain that once you know what it's all about, you'll be able to help him."

It sounds such good sense doesn't it? I wonder if I could volunteer to give it away on the National Health?

"But I don't know you. I mean you've been very kind and nice but—"

"What could be better? You don't want to know me. Just look on me like some kind of doctor who's about to give you an examination."

I squeeze her hand tenderly and pull her towards me. "You make it sound so convincing," she says apologetically. "Oh, I did look forward to it so much before we got married."

"It's not always easy at first," I say, kissing her gently on the cheek. "It's like learning to ride a bike. You have to be prepared to fall off a few times." On reflection that does not seem the best way I could have put it but it is too late to rephrase it now.

"Oh," she says. "You've got a hairy chest. Just like Roger."

"Just think of me *as* Roger," I purr, sliding my arm

69

round her waist. "Close your eyes and imagine that he's come back and is sliding into bed beside you."

"Do you mind drawing the curtains a bit?"

"Nobody can see."

"I know but I feel happier when it's a bit dark. I'm shy, you see."

She is sitting there obediently with her eyes closed so I half draw the curtains, turn the key in the lock, and whip my clothes off so quickly that one of my fly buttons rolls under the wardrobe.

"That's a very pretty nightdress," I murmur as I slide in beside her. "Very pretty."

"I made it myself. Can I open my eyes now?"

"Of course. How do you feel?"

"Frightened."

"That's nothing new, is it?"

"No, I suppose not."

"Well, I'm not frightened, I'm excited." I take her hand and guide it down the front of my body. "Feel."

She touches me gingerly as if trying to remove a piece of cheese from a mousetrap.

"It's huge," she says.

I shake my head sadly. "I wish you were right. It just feels like that because you're not used to it and you can't see it."

"I could never get that inside me."

"Let me worry about that," I kiss her gently on the lips and slip my hand under her nightie.

"Relax. Don't stiffen up. Come on, you're very pretty."

Slowly but surely her tongue darts out and stays pinned between her teeth. Her small breasts seem to grow beneath my hands and her hard nipples quiver expectantly.

"You like that, don't you?"

"Um. Lovely! You have very gentle hands. Are you going to touch me there?"

"In a minute. There's no hurry."

This is not strictly true but I have left the key in the lock in case somebody comes to see what's happened to me.

"Oh, that's heaven."

I run my fingers over her belly and lightly brush against the soft hairs that nestle below it. Tiptoe to the two lips, in fact. Very gently I plough the moist furrow and—

"Oh, be careful."

"This doesn't hurt, does it?"

"A little."

"I'm going to move my finger about a bit. How's that?"

"Alright. In fact it's quite nice, really."

We go on like this for a bit and I am beginning to feel fruitier than Covent Garden. There is a nice pink flush in her cheeks and her eyes are closed contentedly. It must be chronic, if you can't get your end away, mustn't it? You forget what some poor devils have to go through—or not go through as seems more the case.

"I'm going to try it with two, now," says kindly Doctor Lea ."Try and grin and bear it. Remember it's in a good cause."

"Think of Roger."

"That's right. Think of Roger."

"Are you sure we're doing the right thing?"

"Positive. Anyway, it's a bit late to worry about it now, isn't it? Now, we've got this far."

"Ouch!" Her hands close around my wrists. "This is the bit that always hurts."

"I know. But we've got to do it. Come on. Think how nice it's going to be later on."

"I hope you're right. Ouch!"

I pull her close to me and make her move her legs around while I offer encouraging noises. It is all a bit clinical for a bloke of my tastes and I can feel J.T. Superstar beginning to get perplexed. It would be a disaster to do a Roger, wouldn't it? The very thought sends cold shivers down my spine. Luckily, the bird is far from passive as far as the old moaning and groaning goes and this helps to keep me on the boil. I can't stand the ones who lie there as if they are wondering what shade of brown to paint the ceiling.

At last I reckon the time has come to do some real plumbing and I gently lever myself between her legs. Such

71

a tiny bird, she is. Her nose is practically pressing against my belly button.

"Here we go," I say. "Stand by for blast off."

For some reason I think of one of those old-fashioned costume movies with a battering ram being positioned outside the gates of the castle. At least nobody is pouring boiling oil down my neck.

"Ouch! Oh, no! Oh!"

"Hang on, we're nearly there. There!"

"Oh! Oh!! Oh!!!!" Her voice rises in a series of shouts progressing from the pained to the triumphant. "Hurrah!"

"That wasn't too bad, was it?"

"Wasn't too good, either, but thank you very much. You don't know what this means to me."

She puts her little hands around my big end and hugs me to her.

"It's nothing. All part of the room service."

She kisses me warmly on the mouth and together we engage full revs and rocket off into the stratosphere—well, would you believe the bed hopped six inches from the wall?

Yes folks, another satisfied patient learns to live again. Just whistle the Dr. Kildare theme while I put on my Y-fronts.

Despite the fact that I only did it out of sheer goodness of heart, I am a bit choked when her old man rolls up around tea-time. I had anticipated that the patient might need a bit more treatment that evening. I see them sitting there in the lounge with half a plate of digestives, and their little hands creeping into each other, and I think: that's it, Lea, close your casebook, zip up your fly, it's ten bob to a tin of Vaseline that things are going to be alright from now on. Just sit back and wait for your Duke of Edinburgh award.

But, not for the first time in my life, I am wrong. Mrs. R. has a strained expression by supper time and at the breakfast table next morning, there are definite signs of tears. Roger is fiddling with his camera strap. Oh dear. It looks as if all my hard work has gone by the board—or bored maybe. No? You're probably right. Anyway, later that morning Mrs. R. approaches me as I am subjecting the silver to a spot of spit and polish in the deserted dining room.

"No good, huh?" I say, reading her face.

She shakes her head. "If you're like other men, he's not like you. Do you think there's something wrong with him? Maybe he should see a doctor?"

"Don't suggest that to him. That'll turn him right off. No, he just needs a bit of a boost somehow."

As I speak my eyes wander down to the end of the room to where Carmen is bending over to adjust a table leg. Yeah. That chick could defrost your refrigerator by brushing against it. At the back of my horrible little mind an idea begins to lurch forward.

"Banging away with his camera, is he?" I ask.

"Yes, it's the—" she bites back what she was going to say and gives a resigned little shrug. "How long is this likely to go on for?"

"It's only temporary. I'm sure of that, but—"

"But what?"

"Well, just to be on the safe side, we ought to give him a feel-up, or whatever it's called."

"A fillip?"

"Precisely. I mean, you're only here for two weeks, I suppose. You don't want to hang about any longer than you have to."

"But surely you can't do anything to him—I mean physical?"

"Blimey no. What kind of bloke do you think I am? No, there are pills and stuff like that but I don't recommend them. They can get a bit out of control if you know what I mean." I think of the Shermer Rugby Club and my blood runs colder than an Eskimo's chuff.

"So, what then?"

"I haven't quite worked out the details yet, but I think he needs a bit of mental stimulation. He's concentrating on you so much he gets uptight every time he lays a finger on you. If we can broaden his horizons a bit—"

Later that day I get Carmen, June and Audrey on one

73

side and fill them in on my plan of campaign. Being the kind of gay, fun-loving girls they are, they express themselves as being only too glad to oblige. My real stroke of luck is when I find that the apartment next to the Richards' bedroom is falling vacant the following morning. Not only that but there is a connecting door between the two suites and it opens into the Richards' bedroom. My cup over-runneth!

A spot more organisation and next morning finds me gliding up behind Mr. Richards as he makes for the front entrance clasping his Leica as if it is the only thing left in the world.

"Oh, Mr. Richards. Sorry to trouble you but I wonder if I could ask you something?" He shrinks away from me as if the only thing I could be asking him is "Why can't you get it up your old lady?" But luckily my up-bringing has protected me against such crudity.

"I remember your wife talking about your success as a photographer, and I wondered if I could ask you to give us a few tips. When I say 'us' I mean the Cromby Photographic Club. There's one or two of us very interested in still lives."

"Well, that's very flattering. I don't see how I can refuse." Richards looks happy for the first time in days. "Don't get any ideas about me being a great performer, though. Daphne is inclined to exaggerate."

"Daphne?"

"My wife."

"Oh, of course. It's lighting that is the trouble with us. Use of flash. All that kind of thing. If you could give us a few hints on positioning models. I'll get one or two of our members along."

"Delighted. What time would you like me?"

"Let's say midday. Then you can join us for a little drink."

"Delighted. Absolutely delighted."

At five minutes to twelve I have June, Audrey and Carmen draped around the semi-darkened apartment. Audrey is wearing a bikini that looks like two elastic bands with

74

three knots in them and heels so high you could use them for planting potatoes. June is sporting a sheet—cot-size so it does not conceal the fact that she is starkers—and Carmen is wearing a dab of Chanel No. 5 behind the knee caps—nothing else to distract you from her manifold charms. I get her standing in the darkest part of the room and pour half a bottle of brandy into the half bottle of sherry I have nicked from Dennis the barman. If this lot does not get him going, nothing will. Tap, tap! "Come in, Mr. Richards. Very kind of you to come. Is Mrs. Richards joining you?"

"In a minute, I hope. She's suddenly decided she wants to change her dress. Very dark in here, isn't it—Oh, my God!"

I bend down and give June her towel back. "Don't over-do it, dear," I hiss. "Let's get a few drinks inside him first." I turn to Richards. "We're very keen on life work as you can see. I did mention that, didn't I?"

"I can't really remember," says Richards, who is now grabbing an eyeful of Audrey's knockers.

"Drink?"

"Yes please." His hand shoots out and he downs a mixture of sherry and brandy—randy shandy I call it—before you can say Cecil Beaton.

"My goodness me." He gives a little laugh and shakes his head like a boxer trying not to let on that he has been hurt. "Interested in flash work, are you?"

June is giving him a flash already and it is obvious that she has been at the booze while my back was turned. I will have to watch them because they are quite capable of taking what is meant for another.

"Get the flash bulbs out, will you Audrey?" I say non-chalantly. "I'll start oiling Carmen."

"You'll what?" Richards is clearly interested and I give him another slug of randy shandy.

"It brings the body tones up a treat. We've had some wonderful results. This is Carmen, by the way."

The noise made by Richards is like air being sucked into a jet engine. I pick up a bottle of olive oil and pour a little

75

between Carmen's massive knockers. Richards is now making choking noises.

"Do you think I'm standing the right way?" asks Carmen. I think she comes from Walsall and she has a very flat voice—the only thing about her that is.

"Well, I-er-um-er think it's er-um, really a-um a question of um-er-lighting."

"You get on with this," I say pushing the bottle into Richards' hand. "I'll go and check the equipment."

This is not going to take long, because we only have one Instamatic and a roll of black and white film, but I don't tell him that. He is dabbing at Carmen's body like he is varnishing a butterfly's wing.

"Let me fill up your glass," Audrey closes to his side and June brings up the rear—one of the best in Hoverton, I might add.

"I don't know if I should."

"Oh, go on, be a devil. Can you put some on me? No, the oil, I mean."

Richards is starting to pour his drink down the front of Audrey's bikini. He is going even faster than I had expected. Too fast, maybe. We want to leave something for his missus, I try and gently remove his drink, but he avoids my hand and takes another giant slug.

"Remarkable brew, quite remarkable." He empties his glass and slams it down on the table so hard that the stem breaks. But does he notice? Does he fucia! "Let's get on with it, then," he yodels. I think he might mean photography but my worries are groundless. He swills olive oil on his mitts and goes at Carmen's knockers like he is trying to smooth out her chest to plant radishes.

A few moments later he is looking around for more customers. "Next!" he hollers. Audrey's bikini is torn away as if by a great hurricane and all the girls start giggling and closing in for the kill.

"You've got to get your exposures right, eh?" Roger nudges me in the ribs and obviously reckons it is the funniest thing anybody has ever said. "Who cares about the ball, let's get on with the game. To think, that for all those years I was concentrating on my camera."

June has taken umbrage at being left out of the action for so long and presses forward her mouth an inviting inch from Mr. Instamatic. But not for long! Like a lost piglet catching up with its milk supply, he launches himself on to her lips and I can see that in a couple of seconds the whole point of my carefully laid plans will be blunted in another gang bang. Carmen is already beginning to undo Richards' belt and dear, loyal Audrey is fiddling with mine. Get orf! "What about Mrs. Richards?" I pipe above the uproar, pulling her old man off June before they can get any closer involved.

"I thought she was joining us?"

"Oh, yes. Yes, so she was."

He tries to turn back to June but I grab her by the shoulder. "You'd better find out what has happened to her," I say, dragging him towards the door that joins the two apartments. Before he can say any more I have flung it open and bundled him through. There, strictly according to instructions sits Mrs. R. filing her nails on the edge of the bed. She is wearing a black bra and panties set with suspender belt and black silk stockings. Gor!! I am on the point of throwing back Mr. R. and going myself. Luckily, my native sense of decency gets the better of me and closing the door on my impulses I drop to my knees and peer through the keyhole. Well, I want to see that everything is alright, don't I? I need have no fears. Mr. R. falters for a moment, and then his eyes light upon the goodies spread out for him. In three strides, he has swept wifey back on to the bed and is fighting his way out of his trousers like an angry ferret escaping from a paper bag. Mrs. R's panties whip over her heels and like a bee late for an appointment with its queen he whips into the hive before you can say honeypot.

I would like to watch more, but you have to draw the line somewhere, don't you? I wish someone would tell that to Carmen, Audrey and June. Regretfully, I turn away from the keyhole to see Carmen tilting the Randy Shandy bottle to her lips. Oh, no! If they have that lot inside them —I spring to my feet and sprint for the door.

"Oh no you don't!"

"But girls—"

"Getting us all excited and then ratting on us."

"Yes, but. Put me down! Stop doing that!"

"If you're not a good boy, we'll go next door. We've got a fan there."

That was the argument that clinched it. I mean. I could not allow my scheme to be spoilt at the last moment, could I? Let Mr. R. get used to one bird first of all. Then he can build up later.

"Is there anything left in that bottle?" I say as my jeans hit the carpet.

CHAPTER FIVE

I don't see the Richards again until they leave the hotel. Nine days and they never leave their room once! When Mrs. R. sails through the front entrance on her way out, she looks a changed woman. I mean, she looks like a woman! Her old man slips me a fiver and gives me a big wink. "Buy the camera club a drink on me," he says, "they're doing a grand job."

I watch the two of them snuggle down in the back of a taxi and I feel almost moist-eyed with pleasure. Almost, I hasten to add. The last time I cried was when England got beaten by West Germany in Mexico. Oh, that one's good deeds could always be so pleasurably accomplished. I exclude from that statement the last part of the exercise. Exercise! By the cringe. When I finally escape from the Terrible Trio, my willy wonker feels like a tassel that has been in a hassle with an electric fan.

In the next few days I steer clear of the birds and concentrate on my duties. As a waiter I learn how to order up courses that people don't want and put them on one side for consumption later. You would think that in a large hotel there would be plenty of spare grub about but often the staff's food is diabolical and the chefs watch for nicking like hawks. If anybody is going to have a bit of spare, it is going to be them.

My most instructive period is that which I spend with Dennis the barman, or head barman as he prefers to be called. He is a grade one tealeaf and I am certain I only get wise to a fraction of his little dodges. For example: he leaves the spirit measure to soak in a bowl of water. Very hygienic, but every time he picks one up to dish out a drink he makes sure he scoops up some of the water in the bowl so that the booze is diluted and he is getting extra mileage out of every bottle. The number of shots per bottle is an established figure so every tot over the top is money in the barman's pocket. It is also fairly easy to take the odd bottle from the stock room without signing for it. Provided the books usually balance, nobody is going to get too fussed about the occasional discrepancy. And, if you are catering for a party, why not buy a few bottles of booze from the local cash and carry and sell them as well as the hotel's stuff? You make a much bigger profit that way. Again, if you have got a bar going at a private party, and you have to do the accounts afterwards, you have to be dozey not to be able to top up a few bottles with what people have left lying about. This way you don't have to account for so much money and the surplus goes into your own pocket.

The softest touch of all is short-changing people. After a while you can tell at a glance the people who count their change. Any business man buying a large round of drinks for his superiors or potential clients is only going to look at the change in order to select a tip twice the size of the one he normally gives. Some poor jerk taking out a girl he wants to impress is also unlikely to start making a fuss. Whether you add a bit to the cost of a round, or indulge in a spot of short-changing, the chances are that you will rarely be challenged. Dennis's speciality, I observed, was to serve a round of drinks and keep some of the change back under the bill which he held out on the tray for the customer to see. Like as not the customer would push some more change over for a tip and if he did notice a discrepancy, the missing change would appear from under the bill where it had "accidentally" got lodged. Jumbo-sized grovelling from Dennis and a temporary drop in his fringe benefits.

Quite how much Dennis made out of his fiddles I don't know but he was rumoured to own a house in the South of Spain, and keep an expensive flat in London. Working with him made me realise that you can never put a stop to all the fiddles but, at least, you can get a bloody good idea of what to look out for if you ever have the misfortune to try and control some of the fly boys who hang out in the hotel business. The trouble is that if you sack one, you stand a good chance of getting someone even worse next time. And it could take you months to get to know all his fiddles! That is what Sid decides anyway, and I reckon he is probably right.

Incidentally, one last word while I am on the subject of fiddles. If you order a gin and tonic or a whisky and dry ginger and it arrives with half the mixer slopped into it, send it back and tell the barman you would rather mix your own drink. Chances are that he has given you a half measure of spirit and topped up with tonic.

Although Sid has fallen for Miss Ruperts' upper crust charms and is prepared to tolerate Mrs. Caitley because of her, he has definitely got the needle with Superpouf, the head waiter, and it is fortunate that the spaghetti bolognese incident brings matters to a head—literally as it turns out.

As already reported, Mrs. Caitley takes umbrage when-ever Bentley tries to step into her sphere of influence and he is taking his life in his hands when he decides that it will be easier to serve the spaghetti bolognese if it is premixed in the kitchen. Mrs. Caitley says no. Ladle the spaghetti out on to the plate, then add the meat sauce from a gravy boat. I would not be fussed either way, but when Super-pouf waits until Mrs. C. has been called to Miss Ruperts' office and invades the kitchen it is like asking for his stamp collection.

I sense something unpleasant is going to happen when he comes staggering out of the kitchen with a great tureen of gunge in his hands. His face is pink and it is obvious that the kitchen staff have said a few nasty things to him.

I tighten my grip on my parmesan as he slaps the bowl down on a serving table and waves at one of the chefs du rang to get on with it. The dining room is pretty crowded by Cromby standards and in view of what is about to happen this is bad luck for everybody. As the chef du rang is about to start serving, the swing doors to the kitchen burst open. It might be a water buffalo but—even more terrifying—it is Mrs. Caitley. The expression on her face makes me shrink back against the wall. Always a close contender with Miss Ruperts for the world's ugliest woman title she is now threatening to break clear of the field. One glance at her mush and I feel like I am standing at the mouth of a cave with a tiger cub under my arm just as mummy gets back from the butchers. Her eye falls on Bentley like a factory chimney collapsing and she eats up the distance between them in half a dozen giant paces.

"Return to your province, Mrs. Caitley," squeals Superpouf retreating from the table.

"Odious toad," hisses Mrs. C. "To set foot in my kingdom is to declare war. How dare you interfere with my arrangements!"

These words are delivered in what I believe is called a stentorian bellow and every bod in the dining room freezes with his fork half way to his cake-hole.

"I am responsible for how the food is served," sniffs Bentley. "Return at once or I will have my staff eject you." If I am supposed to be one of his staff he can count me out. I would not back Joe Frazier against Mrs. C. Current form proves me right as she feints to jab and then throws a left hook which explodes on the point of Bentley's jaw.

"Seize her," he howls, staggering backwards. There is a half-hearted shuffle from those more courageous than myself, but before any action can be taken Mrs. C. has snatched up the tureen of pre-mixed Spaghetti Bolognese.

"If this is what you want, you can have it," she howls.

Whoosh!!! Everybody within twenty feet gets a helping and if they want seconds then Bentley is the man to come to. He is covered in the stuff and his eyes blink out like he is trapped in a cage of spaghetti.

You have to laugh but before I can get into my stride the swing doors to the kitchen burst open and reinforcements arrive. As I have said before Caitley's Corps tend to be on the rough side and this lot do not look as if they are on their way to the Badminton Horse Trials. Crunch! Biff! Wallop! Before further words can be spoken they wade into the waiters and the guests have to fend for themselves. The bright ones scarper while others cower at their tables and two effeminate coves, trapped in a corner, slide under the table cloth at floor level.

There is never much love lost between waiters and kitchen staff and anybody who does not believe me should be standing in the dining room of the Cromby at this moment —preferably behind a sheet metal screen. Spaghetti Bolognese—mixed and separate—is flying in all directions, usually still in a container, and the walls look like the site of an action painting contest. Tables collapse under the weight of the bodies struggling on them and shouts and screams of pain and fury fill the air. Many old scores are being settled and when I see Superpouf staggering past with a soup tureen wedged down over his lugholes I reckon it must be game, set and match to Mrs. Caitley. Surely this little lot will spell finito for both of them. What a wonderful opportunity for Sidney to start swinging his axe.

Crunch! The table in the corner goes and the two lank coves scuttle out holding hands. One of them is clasping a yellow wig to his chest like a woman clinging to her jewels as she leaves a burning house. Yes, it must be goodbye Bentley, goodbye Mrs. C.

But, not a bit of it. Superpouf gets marching orders or resigns—there is some doubt as to which—but Mrs. Caitley remains firmly in command of the kitchen.

"She's done a good job," says Sid when I complain. "We won't get anyone better. Also, she has this special relationship with Miss Ruperts."

"You mean they're a couple of old—"

"No need for any of that Timmo," says Sid reproachfully. "I am referring to their working relationship."

"Get rid of both of them. They're useless."

"They know the business, Timmo."

"They've been giving you the business ever since we got here, Sid! What do you need them for? Anyone could make a better job of running this place. With all your Funfrall experience you could do it standing on your head."

Sid looks haughty. "I am not trying to run a Funfrall operation. Something classier than that. I think Miss Ruperts has the contacts to help me. I've been discussing an idea with her."

"Selling up?" I say, hopefully.

"Don't take the piss, Timmo. No, I was considering the possibility of catering for specialist groups. Conventions, clubs, conferences. That kind of thing. That way we could guarantee filling the hotel and making a few bob on fringe activities, dances, cocktail parties. See what I mean?"

I hate to admit it but Sid does seem to have the germ of an idea there. He interprets my silence correctly.

"Not bad, is it? We could make quite a name for ourselves."

"Anything would be better than the Cromby. When are we going to change that?"

Sid looks shifty. "Well, Miss Ruperts has a great sentimental attachment to the name and—"

"Oh, forget it, Sid. She's got you completely under her thumb. When are you going to tell Rosie about it?"

Sid does not care for that remark and before I can ask him more about his plans we engage in a swift verbal punch-up which leads to me being banished to assist Martin the hall porter, commissionaire and octogenarian. This man is so past it he has to get the guests to help him carry the room keys up two flights of stairs and has been known to sit on their bed for five minutes to recover.

I am pacing up and down trying to keep out of the draught when a car squeals to a halt outside and three smartly-dressed middle-aged men sporting red carnations in their buttonholes leap out. One of them is carrying a large bunch of flowers. They ignore me and press forward to Miss Primstone.

"I believe you have a suite reserved for Mr. and Mrs. Beecham?" says one of them.

Miss Primstone never has any problem hearing upper class voices and checks her register.

"Yes. The Pallgrave Suite."

"Excellent," purrs Smoothie-Chops. "They should be here any minute. From the registry office."

He winks conspiratorially and Miss Primstone switches on her "Oh, young love", expression.

'We've got a few flowers we'd like to decorate their rooms with."

"Well, I don't know. If you leave them with me—"

"I know you'd do it quite beautifully." Smoothie-Chops' smile would melt concrete.

"But it's the messages. We haven't got much time. They're going to be here any minute."

I don't like the way the tall gangling one is giggling through his stained teeth but Miss Primstone does not seem to notice that.

"Oh, all right then. I shouldn't really be doing this." She reaches behind her for the key.

"You're too kind."

They brush past her, look for the lift like so many before them, and disappear up the stairs.

"Second floor, turn right," calls Miss Primstone after them. She turns to me and shakes her head. "That's the class of person we used to have all the time in the old days." She says the words as if she blames me for the fact that they don't come any more.

I shrug my shoulders and walk away, because they don't do anything for me and I don't want to be drawn into any agrochat. Five minutes later they rush past us again and Stained-Teeth is splitting his sides. I don't like it. I don't like it at all.

"I think I'll go up and have a look," I say, heading for the stairs.

"You're a fine one to be suspicious," sniffs Miss Primstone. I consider pushing her into one of the pigeon holes but eventually decide against it.

"It's a change to have a couple staying here you know are married," she continues.

Poor old Miss P. I am certain she is dying for a bit and will die before she gets it. I wish I was man enough to put her out of her misery. Maybe I could get Martin pissed one night. No, the stupid old sod is past it, too.

Before I can set foot on the stairs, there is a commotion in the hall and a distinguished grey-haired bloke enters, labouring under the weight of a suitcase. He is accompanied by a well-developed lady of mature charms wearing a too-tight two-piece. She has what I think is an orchid in her buttonhole and he sports another red carnation.

"Leave it, Henry. Leave it," she drawls in a strong American accent. "The boy will handle it. What are you trying to prove? You won't have the strength to carry me over the threshold if you go on like this." No prizes for guessing who they are.

The woman walks over to the reception and writes something in the dust. "Gee," she says, her eyes probing the gloom. "They said this was a delightful small watering place. I wouldn't water a mule here."

Miss Primstone pretends she does not hear and pushes forward the register.

"Mr. and Mrs. Beecham?"

"Jesus!" exclaims Mrs. B. "Did they see the label on your plasma bottle?"

Mr. B. grinds out a grin. "Can't keep anything a secret, can you?" When you get him in the light he looks a lot older than her and the dark bags under his eyes have dark bags under them. Mrs. B. may not be joking about the plasma.

"Are you going to help my husband to carry those cases?" she says. "I don't think he's going to be much use to me if he has to drag them over to the elevator."

I decide that this is a bad moment to tell her we don't have an elevator and bring the rest of the cases in. It is noticeable that she has about six spanking new leather jobs and he one battered "I saw Port Harcourt and lived" type. I imagine that he must have some kind of appeal that is not immediately noticeable to the eye.

"I wish you'd told me we were coming to this place, doll," says Mrs. B. wearily as we toil up the stairs. "And I'd have told you we weren't. Did Queen Elizabeth sleep here? Or was it your first wife?"

"Place has changed a bit," pants hubby. "It's very difficult to find anywhere at this time of year."

"It must be difficult to find a place like this, twice." Mrs. B. looks me up and down, checking my physique. "Don't go too far, boy. I may need you. I haven't climbed so many stairs since I visited the Great Boulder Dam."

We get to the door of the apartment and I fling it open—or rather, I try and fling it open, the hinges are a bit rusty.

"Gee," says Mrs. B. sarcastically. "What a pretty shade of brown. Who told you it was my favourite colour?" She collects some more dust on the fingers of her white glove. "And, do you know, Henry. I think they've left everything just as it was from the time Queen Elizabeth slept here."

She turns to me. "Have you got a telephone? I think I'll try and ring the Grand."

I am busy looking round the room to see if the three jokers have been up to anything, but nothing seems to have been tampered with. The flowers must be in the bedroom.

"The telephone is in the bedroom, modom," I say and open the door.

Mrs. B. peers inside. "The bed is more like it," she says, perking up. "Room for Henry the Eighth and all his wives, huh?" The bed is indeed built on the grand scale and I am relieved to find it flanked by two vases of flowers.

Hubby is also relieved. "There we are, my dear. I knew you wouldn't be disappointed."

"That remains to be seen," says the new Mrs. B. pointedly. "Where did those flowers come from? I think somebody thought we were getting buried, not married."

Now she comes to mention it, there do seem to be a lot of lilies and other funereal blooms.

"It's the thought that counts," murmurs Mr. B.

"That's what worries me. I bet they came from your first wife."

I am about to explain about the three gentlemen when Mr. Beecham decides to sit on the bed. He tests its softness with his hand, gives it a pat, then turns and sits down. I remember the smile of premature satisfaction on his face as he sinks down—and down. The jokers have unscrewed the bedstead and the poor old geezer lands up on the floor with his legs in the air. There is the sound of a chamber pot shattering and a cloud of dust fills the room.

"My God," says Mrs. B. springing back. "What did I tell you? It folds into an instant coffin."

Before she can say any more, Mr. B.'s groans alert us to the fact that he really has hurt himself and, eventually, when we have prised Dr. McDonald away from his bottle of Scotch, we discover that the poor bloke has a badly slipped disc and must go to hospital. On his wedding night, too. What a tragedy!

At first Mrs. B. threatens to sue everybody up to the Duke of Edinburgh but we quieten her down and explain what happened and she decides to concentrate her wrath on the three blokes concerned, one of whom, of course, turns out to be the bridegroom's best man. They nicked the flowers from a local graveyard. Oh well, I expect it seemed a good idea at the time.

On her return from the hospital Mrs. B., or Sadie as I learn she is called, tries to book in at the Grand and the Imperial but they are both full. Thwarted in her attempt to escape, she retires to her apartment and orders a bottle of Bourbon to be sent up.

"And send the cute one," she says, meaning me.

When I get there she has taken her jacket off and is revealing a shapely pair of bristols lunging against a halter neck jumper.

"Put it down there," she says meaning the tray. "Boy, I wasn't expecting too much, but I was hoping for better than this."

"I'm very sorry," I say. "The bed is all right now, isn't it?"

"Do you think we should check it? No, don't look so alarmed. I was only joking. Tell me, what's a good-looking boy like you doing in a place like this?"

"It belongs to my brother-in-law. He's just taken it over."

"He should try taking it over the side of a cliff. I wouldn't put up my last husband in a dump like this."

I don't have an answer for that and she pulls a packet of cigarettes out of her handbag.

"I expect you're asking yourself what a beautiful dame like me is doing getting hitched to Beecham when I could have my pick of any man in the world." She watches my adam's apple as I swallow. "You're right. I'm lonely. Nobody wants to marry people of my age. Take them out, sleep with them, sure. But I want someone to talk to in the long winter evenings. In a few years I'm going to have problems finding three clean old ladies to play bridge with. Do you know how many times I've been married?"

I shake my head.

"This is the fourth. Four times. The only one I loved gave me one night of heaven and the next morning there was just a hole in the bed where he had been. I never saw him again. He took everything I had—even my clothes—I loved that bastard." She glugs some more Bourbon into her tumbler. "You don't know what to say, do you? Have a drink, it'll loosen your tongue."

"No thanks. I think I'd better be getting along."

"You're a shy boy, aren't you?" The truth is that with her I am. Give me some innocent little scrubber who says "Oh, Timmy you're smashing. I don't half fancy you" and I am all over her. But this bird has had four husbands—well, three and a half, anyway—and talks as if she could eat three of me for breakfast. I feel Percy slinking away with his tail between my legs, and make for the door.

"I'll take dinner in the apartment," she says grandly. "And you'd better bring it up."

Just as long as you don't, I think to myself as I go downstairs. It is Mrs. Caitley's night off and the bloke who stands in would be pushed to win a cooking contest against my mum. I have seen him turning over an egg in his hand as if looking for the instructions.

That afternoon I have a swim and report back to the hotel about six-thirty. Sure enough, Sadie has phoned down her order and asked for it to be brought to her room by me at eight o'clock sharp.

"I theenk mybe I shoulda handle theez one myself," says the new Head Waiter who is (would you believe?) Italian and obviously very hot on the frippet.

"No, no, Senor Luigi," I lie. "I promised her old man I would see she was all right. I'd better do as she says."

"But I have much experience of American ladies."

I bet you do, mate, I think to myself. Three coins in the fountain—and about forty-eight pairs of knickers.

In the end I practically have to wrench the tray away from him. I mean, I don't reckon anything is going to happen, but if by chance it does, I want it to happen to me and not to some blooming Eyetie.

I run a moist finger along my eyebrows and tap on the door. I have a feeling that Sadie will be spread out on the bed wearing a long frilly negligee, but I am wrong. She is standing by the repaired bed and gazing down at a long frilly negligee that is lying on top of it.

"Beautiful, isn't it?" she says as I cough discreetly in the doorway. "Too bad he isn't going to see it for a few days. I suppose I could wear it round to the hospital under a long coat. Whip it open and whee! They don't have lady flashers, do they?"

I shake my head. "I've never seen one. Where are you going to eat?"

"Oh, put it down over there. It's not going to get cold, is it?" She is right there because everything she has ordered is from the cold plate. A wise choice as I have already indicated. "Now—what's your name?"

"Lea—Timothy Lea."

"Well, Tim . . . I'd like you to join me in a drink. You do have a few moments, don't you? It's my wedding night and I want to have a good time!" She looks away and bites her lip and for a moment I think I am going to have to whip out the handkerchief again. Blimey, but you need to be a man of many parts in this game. Guide, philosopher and fiend as Ted Hotchkiss used to say at Melody Bay.

"That's very kind of you. Thanks."

A glance at the liquid left in the bourbon bottle tells me that it has been sinking faster than the country's gold reserves. Mrs. Beecham has obviously been drinking to forget her sorrows. Not that I blame her. A wedding night with Mr. B. would not be my idea of the first prize on the back of a cornflakes packet, but it is better than being on your tod.

"He was all right, was he?" I say conversationally.

"Henry? Do you mean in the sack or when I saw him in hospital? Oh, sorry. You're blushing again. Yes, he seemed O.K. He couldn't move much but his stiff upper lip was still bend-proof. I suppose that's one of the things that appealed to me about the guy when I first met him. That and his background. He's very well connected, you know." She smiles. "I mean, family-wise. Practically an aristocrat. That's what I need, a touch of class." She runs a finger lightly down my nose. "Have you got class?"

"Not that kind."

"No, you're more the noble savage type, aren't you? Do you get pestered by lots of ladies?"

"Not as far as the paying customers are concerned. Most of them have to be lifted into their bath chairs."

"What a shame. You want to get a job in a cruise boat —or somewhere in the south of France. That way your talents could be really exploited."

"I don't have any trouble being exploited. My brother-in-law is an expert at it."

Mrs. B. looks as if she is about to say something, and then changes her mind.

"He drives you hard, huh?"

"Yes. He's going to make a million before he's finished."

Mrs. B. helps herself to another shot and, as an after-thought, tosses the remainder of the bottle into my glass.

"Do you know what I'd like to do now?"

There is a faint flush about her throat which may have something to do with the twenty-six fluid ounces of booze inside her and her not inconsiderable tits are jostling each other to get at me. Yes, I do know what she would like to do now.

"No," I say innocently.

"I'd like to lay you," she says fervently. "I'd like to take your firm young body and give it the fruits of my years of experience."

I should be jumping up and down and clapping my hands together but the minute she starts talking about years of experience I begin to get nervous again. What was nice about Mrs. Daphne Richards was that I was in control. I was giving her the fruits of my years of experience. Too often these days, I am being used as a sort of dildo on legs. I must write to my M.P. about it when I get a moment.

"Take off that ridiculous little jacket," says Mrs. Beecham. "It's too tight for you across the shoulders."

"Thanks for the drink," I say. "Ring when you want the tray picked up."

Mrs. B.'s eyes open wide. "What's the matter. Don't you want me?"

"It's not that."

"Are you queer, or something?"

"No, of course I'm not. I just don't like being taken for granted, that's all."

"But baby—" She comes towards me and slides her arms round my neck.

"Mrs. Beecham. You're drunk and you'd be better off in bed—alone." I don't mean to sound so pious but once I get into my stride there is no holding me. It is as if I am getting the satisfaction I might have got in bed from being unkind to her. Vere interestink, eh, Herr Doctor?

I remove her hands and turning on my heel, make for the door. Immediately, Mrs. B. bursts into tears. "Don't leave me," she sobs. "Not now, I couldn't stand it. I'm sorry if I offended you. I just need to be with someone. I don't want to be alone." She collapses on to a sofa and the whole upper part of her body is shaking in time with her

91

sobs. Very impressive it is, too. The minute she starts doing that my whole attitude changes. My frustrated desire to dominate is unlumbered and a happy urge to rip her knickers off flows through my system. Any bird who starts crying when I am around stands a good chance of making an appointment with Percy. Nasty, aren't I? Careful! I heard that.

"Why don't you have something to eat?" I say not unkindly. "I looked out a nice piece of turkey for you." I extend an arm and take her hand but she does not move; just squeezes my fingers tight. I sit down beside her and tilt her head up.

"Come on, cheer up. I'm sorry, too. I know how you must feel. I came over a bit narky, that's all." I take out my handkerchief—there's posh for you—which by some miracle is fairly clean and start dabbing at the make-up smudges under her eyes.

"You look as if you work in a coal mine." It is not the funniest joke ever made, but it raises a smile.

"Stop crying, I can't keep up with you."

She is beginning to relax a bit now. Still quivering, but blinking fast to stop the flow of tears. Women in such a condition give off a very back-to-nature pong which turns me on like the Blackpool Illuminations. I can feel myself wilting. No, not wilting. That is completely the wrong word. I can feel my determination to push off disappearing faster than Ted Heath's re-election prospects. The rest of me is coming on strong.

"There, that's better." Suddenly, I am doing all the talking.

"Thank you."

We sit in silence for a moment and then something not entirely unrelated to nooky-craving makes me kiss her gently on the lips. Oh, the taste of tears and the smell of booze. A very stirring combination.

"Are you going to go?"

"I'll think about it."

Slowly I slide my arm about her and draw her into the hollow of my shoulder. Our mouths get better acquainted and my greedy fingers plunder her bristols. She slips her hand inside my shirt and grabs hold of any spare flesh she can find. Luckily there is some, otherwise I would not be able to bend down and tie up my shoe laces. We continue like this for a few happy minutes and then my restless fingers are on the move again. Five stubby soldiers of fortune heading into the great known. Under cover of her skirt they set to with a will while Sadie responds to their advances with delighted moans. You have to work long hours in this job, but it does have its fringe benefits. Mrs. B. sighs and sends down a pandy to check on my own movements.

"Aren't those pants a bit tight for you?" she observes.

She is dead right and they are getting tighter every minute.

"Let's go next door. It's more comfortable."

We uncouple and, when I throw open the bedroom door, the bed is illuminated in a pool of light. Standing beside it we help each other off with our clothes smacking our lips at the thought of what is to come. Sadie wriggles against my chest and gently tugs down my pants while I unhook her bra.

"Don't put the light on," she murmurs. "I'm an old woman. I don't want you to see my body."

"An *older* woman," I reassure her. "There's a lot of difference."

She falls back across the bed and I lie down beside her feeling the cool satin counterpane against my back. She is a very curvy lady.

"Can we get inside the bed?" she says. "Please. It's cold."

She is right. The central heating which makes a noise like a tank regiment advancing through wooded country has been turned off from just before the cold spell in May. One thing about the Cromby, they do a very nice bed. Eiderdowns, counterpanes, the lot. Very snug you feel with that on top of you. That and Mrs. Beecham pressing in on you like an inspirational new hot water bottle design.

"Oh, baby," she breathes. "Baby, baby, baby!"

I think I have mentioned before that some of my happiest moments have been spent in the company of those ladies who have taken advantage of the advancing years to gather a rich harvest of experience and Mrs. B. is no exception. She also has a great deal of typical Yank enthusiasm. A high-spirited "get up and go" approach which I have to prevent matching with a "get up and come". I am also conscious that I am performing for England and to a lesser extent, Mr. Beecham. Also that this is Mrs. B.'s wedding night. Quite a weight of responsibility for young shoulders to bear but fortunately I find myself more than equal to the task.

"Oh baby," she breathes. "I feel beautiful."

"You're right, you're right," I echo. We thunder on, forging Anglo-American relations with every hammer blow, until Mrs. B. starts fizzing like a Catherine Wheel and we both break out into what seems like the end piece of a Fourth of July firework display.

It is while I am gulping in mouthfuls of air and listening to my heart thumping as if it is being played in stereo with the bass turned up that I become aware that someone is banging on the door of the apartment. Mrs. Beecham has also heard, because her giant knockers loom above me as she sits up in bed.

"Oh, F-f-fuxbridge."

"Don't worry," says Mrs. B. sliding out of bed and grabbing a robe. "I'll see who it is."

"Tell them I nipped out to buy some aspirins," I call after her. I snuggle back in the sheets, pleasantly exhausted and look forward to Sadie's return. It is very satisfying to turn someone on like that. Not bad on the strictly personal level, either. I hear Mrs. B. drawling away to someone and then the door closing. Good. Then a male voice approaching. Bad! I am half-way under the sheets when the bed-room door is pushed open.

"Henry," calls Mrs. B. "Oh, Henry, I've got a surprise for you." Whoever she means, she can't be kidding. Before I can do anything, a big guy with a crewcut is walking towards the bed with his hand outstretched. I examine it closely to see if there is a gun nestling in it. Luckily it is empty.

"You could probably kill me for bursting in at a moment like this." He is right. "But I was passing through on my

94

way back to the States and I bumped into one of Sadie's buddies at the airport. You could have knocked me down with a feather." I would prefer to use a sledgehammer and do the job properly. "I put my flight back a few hours, hired a car and here I am. Couldn't miss the opportunity to pay my respects to dear old Sadie and her new Mr. Right. Put it there, pardner."

"Pleased to meet you. Ouch!" I say as the Yank crushes my knuckles in his giant mitt.

"I hear you're some kind of noble?"

"Um, well in a manner of speaking I—er," I mumble trying to move my accent up three social classes. Sadie comes to the rescue swiftly.

"Hiram! You just don't ask questions like that over here. It's bad enough pushing me out of the way and rushing into the bedroom on our wedding night."

"I'm sorry, honey. I didn't mean no offence. It's just that I feel I have some special rights as far as you're concerned. After all, we were married."

"But only for five weeks, Hiram. It doesn't give the right to rush in here like its a press show."

"Don't get mad at me, honey. And, you sir, please forgive me. I only wanted to say howdy do and bring you your present." He dives into his pocket and produces what looks like a handful of silver fire.

"Hiram! It's beautiful."

"I got it back from my fifth wife last week and I don't really want it. I'd like you to have it. You were my favourite, Sadie. Too bad we married too young."

"But you were forty-two, Hiram."

"I was slow maturing. Anyhow, I'm glad you like it," he turns back to me. "Delighted to have made your acquaintance, sir. I hope I weather half as well as you. I was expecting you to be much older."

"I'm working at it."

"Very amusing, sir. Well, I must be off. I'm still living in the old place, Sadie. So when you're both in New York you must look me up."

"That's real nice of you, Hiram."

95

"Absolutely topping." I say, deciding he deserves a slice of genuine upper class lingo.

"So long."

"'Bye."

"Toodle pip!"

The great toilet brush goes out and gives an Oliver Hardy wave as he closes the door gently behind him.

"Blimey, I hope he doesn't bump into your Henry."

"It's very unlikely, sweetheart. If he does, he'll think you were another husband."

She fastens the necklace round her neck and studies herself in the wardrobe mirror. It hangs down in layers like chain mail.

"Do you think it suits me?"

I come up behind her and ease the robe off her shoulder so that she is naked again. "I think you set it off a treat."

She turns and her big, warm body presses against mine. Her hands start to go up to her neck but I pull them down again.

"Keep it on," I say. "And get on to that bed."

"Alright, Henry. Anything you say."

CHAPTER SIX

"Hey, you. Where can I find Noggett?"

It is a week after the Beechams have left—he looking a bit worse than when he went into hospital; God knows what she was doing to the poor old sod—and I am standing in for Sandra who is having a bash on the tennis court—or more likely—in the long grass behind it! Every time she comes back she is covered in burrs. Everywhere but on her knickers, as I found out once when she bent down. Funny, that.

The bloke who is addressing me is about my age and has shoulder-length hair worn over the collar of his smart suit. He is carrying a pig-skin attaché case. Apart from his manner I don't like his shifty eyes which are darting round the foyer as if trying to memorise every feature.

"Do you mean 'Mr. Noggett'?" I say primly.

"There's only one, isn't there?" The tone is only slightly less than a snarl.

"I'll see if he is available. Who shall I say wants to see him?"

"Edward Rigby." The bloke is now tapping the walls. "And hurry up, will you? I'm a busy man. I haven't got time to hang around this morgue."

When I find Sidney he is in Miss Ruperts' office cocking his little finger over a cup of tea.

"Miss Ruperts has surpassed herself," he pipes. "The Pendulum Society are going to hold their convention here. Every room in the hotel booked Friday to Sunday. Isn't she a clever girl?" Sidney coming the smarmer makes me want to puke, but I manage to control myself. "Great," I say. "There's a nasty looking Herbert in the foyer who wants to speak to you. He didn't say what it was about."

"Oh, well, better see him, I suppose."

I notice, as we leave, that Miss Ruperts has a bottle of brandy under the tea cosy. She does not change.

When we get into the foyer, Rigby looks Sid up and down like he is measuring him for a coffin.

"Mr. Noggett?"

"That's right. What can I do for you?"

"I'd like to have a few words with you—in private."

He looks at me like I came off the bottom of his shoe after a walk around Battersea Dogs' Home.

"Mr. Lea is my personal assistant. You can speak freely in front of him."

Blimey! It is a long time since Sidney referred to me like that. He must obviously find this cove as unlovable as I do.

Rigby shrugs and we go into Sid's office.

"Let me come to the point at once," says Rigby, hardly waiting till his arse has hit the chair before he starts speaking. "I've come round here to offer you a fair price for this place. I'm in property and I want to develop this site. I've bought the freeholds on either side of you and I hope we can come to a sensible arrangement."

"What if we can't?" says Sid.

"I don't think there's a lot of alternative. I'm going to start demolishing both the buildings on either side of you in a few weeks and I'll be surprised if that does anything for your business—if you have any." This guy's money obviously ran out half way through charm school.

"What kind of figure were you thinking of?"

Rigby mentions a figure which makes me want to scream "grab it and run!" but Sid does not bat an eyelid.

"That's ridiculous," he says. "It cost me more than that."

"Take it or leave it."

"I'll leave it."

Rigby produces a card and drops it on the table in front of Sid. "When you've had time to reconsider, or talked it over with someone who knows the business, get in touch with me."

"The council won't let you start pulling down the buildings next door."

"They're all in favour of it. This end of town is going downhill so fast they'd like to put it on wheels and push it along the coast." He stands up. "Don't leave it too long. I'll start reducing my offer at the end of the week."

"Piss off." Sid's words may be less than eloquent, but they sum up our feelings more than adequately.

"No need to take that tone. I—"

"PISS OFF!" Sid jumps out of his chair and Rigby has his hand on the door knob quicker than Mary Whitehouse adjusting the picture control on her tele when a naughty bit comes along.

"Jumped up little basket," snarls Sid when Rigby has disappeared.

"Do you think he was bluffing, Sid?"

Sid walks over to the window and pulls back the curtain. Outside we can see Rigby climbing into a chauffeur-driven Rolls.

"No," he says. He picks up Rigby's card. "'Rigram Property Company'. I've heard of them. I think Sir Giles had something to do with them at Funfrall."

"He's done all right for himself, that bloke, hasn't he? He didn't look any older than me."

"Yeah. Make's you sick, doesn't it?"

"What are we going to do, Sid?"

Sid takes a deep breath. "I'm going to make a few enquiries at the Town Hall. And then I'm going to concentrate on getting things ready for the Pendulum Society. We must not be diverted from our purpose, Timmo. Rigby or no Rigby, I intend to make this place posh and profitable."

"Did you really pay more than he offered for this place?"

"I exaggerated a bit, but it was still a pitiful price he came up with. You don't know how much I put myself in hock to get this lot. Considering that we crept in just before the boom, he should have given me a much better deal. Anyhow," his face brightens, "don't let's look on the gloomy side any more. I'm really chuffed about this Pendulum scene. The family is coming down next weekend and I want them to see the place looking as if it's got a bit of life about it."

"You mean Rosie and Jason?"

"Your mum and dad, and all. I couldn't leave them out, could I?"

I know what answer I would have given. Mum and Dad always spell trouble. I would have thought that Sid would have sussed that after his experiences on the Isla de Amor.

Sid is well pleased because the Pendulum mob want to have a dance on the Saturday night and he reckons that we stand to make a few bob from the catering. About half as much as Dennis, I reckon.

As Friday gets nearer, Sidney burns around the hotel getting up everybody's bracket in a big effort to make the staff respond like Funfrall employees. In this endeavour he is wasting his time. All their get up and go got up and went years ago and only highly strung Sandra buckles to with a will—or, as I personally suspect, a willy. One afternoon, I notice a lot of burrs around Sid's turnups and I reckon it is he who has been giving her a quick in and out behind

99

the tennis courts. Better keep that lot under control when the family gets here.

Friday afternoon comes and the first delegates—as Sidney chooses to call them—begin to roll up. I notice that they all seem to be married couples, or sign in as married couples, and are a bit smarter and younger than our normal guests. Early middle-aged trendy with a fair sprinkling of love beads and the like on the men.

"What is this Pendulum Club?" I ask Miss Primstone who is watching the new arrivals disapprovingly.

"I have no idea," she says coldly. "They are certainly not the kind of people I would have expected to find here in the old days. I don't know what has come over Miss Ruperts. It must be the influence of your Mr. Noggett." I would have thought it was the other way round myself, but I don't say anything.

One thing I do notice about the Pendulum mob is that they seem very affectionate with each other. Lots of hugging and kissing on the cheek and long burning glances. It does not look like the Labour Party conference at all.

"Sid, what is this Pendulum Club?" I ask later on.

"Dunno. Some kind of friendly society, I think."

"They're friendly all right. They can hardly keep their hands off each other."

This is nowhere truer than in relation to a bloke called Sam—Sam the Ram soon becomes our name for him. This geezer is about six and a half foot tall and has a silver goatee beard, enormous hooter and hands like seal's flippers. He is constantly rubbing birds into his chest like embrocation and threatening to explode out of the front of his too-tight pink and white toreador pants. If he turned round quickly the weight of junk hanging round his neck could take your head off, and hair sprouts from the top of his open-necked shirt like black foam.

The birds seem to lap all this up and I notice that June and Audrey are not slow to show their appreciation.

"Smashing," says June.

"Smashing," says Audrey. "I bet he's got a big one."

By the time the gong goes for dinner, it takes a performance like the opening of a J. Arthur Rank film to break through the noise coming from the cocktail lounge. I have never seen the place so full.

"What time are the family getting here?" I ask Sid, thinking how impressed they would be to see the place jammed with gay fun-lovers.

Sid looks glum. "I've just had a telephone call from Rosie. Jason has been sick and they won't be coming until tomorrow."

"That's a pity. Still, they'll be here for the dance won't they?"

"Yeah. That should be quite an affair if it goes anything like this." Never has Sidney spoken a truer word.

When we eventually get them in to supper I notice that a good many of the husbands and wives have split up and are not sitting together. I suppose they must have known each other before they got here. I notice, too, that they all have a gong-like medal strung round their necks. It must have something to do with the pendulum bit. At the end of the meal Sam the Ram scrapes back his chair and addresses the throng.

"Get in tune with your surroundings, people," he intones. "The Mellow Mingle will begin at two hours before tomorrow. Keys please, to the ballroom where nightcaps will be served and friendships cemented." He flicks the gong round his neck so that it swings from side to side, and sits down as an interested murmur spreads around the room. Swings. Pendelum. Swings. Swingers! By the cringe! I take another good look around the nuzzling diners and there can be no doubt about it. They are wife-swappers to a man. Husband-swappers to a woman. Does Sidney know what he has let himself in for? Surely Miss Ruperts cannot have been party to this unsavoury flesh-trading. The diners began to drift away and I flee to Sidney's side.

"They're all bleeding wife-swappers," I gasp. "Did you know that?"

"Funny you should say that. The same thoughts was going through my mind." Sid does not sound very concerned.

"What are you going to do about it?"

"What do you expect me to do about it? Tell them all to leave? I don't care what they get up to as long as it doesn't frighten the staff."

"Or the residents."

"Oh, yes. I'd forgotten about them, well, they're all so ga ga they wouldn't notice if Mrs. Caitley started doing a striptease."

"Don't be so disgusting! I bet the whale bone in her corsets was turning yellow when Moby Dick was a tadpole."

"Be your age, Timmo. You're so old fashioned sometimes. Having a bit on the side isn't the sin it used to be. A very nice class of person indulges these days you know."

"That makes it all right then doesn't it? Blimey, Sidney Noggett, you're the biggest snob I know. Anything is all right if you read about it in Nova."

"I don't know what you're on about. All I know is that the hotel is full and that none of them signed the register with x's. That's good enough for me."

"Well, I hope Rosie sees it like that." Then, at last, Sidney's face registers a trace of disquiet.

I have a few hours off that evening so I slip into my dudes and nip out for a drink; I can't afford the prices at the Cromby. As I sit in the snug at the Fisherman's Arms and consider the design on the beer mats, it occurs to me that Sidney's attitude may well be the right one. It also occurs to me that there is a lot of spare back at the hotel and that I do not have an old lady to worry about. I mean, I am all in favour of free love, but I can't imagine my wife ever being ready for it. They take things so much more seriously than us don't they? Look at Rosie with Ricci Volare on the Isla de Amòr. She still stiffens every time Jimmy Young plays Come Prima.

I knock back my drink and whip round to the hotel. It is five to ten and I just have time to squirt some after-shave down the front of my Y-fronts before joining the crowd pushing into the ballroom. None of the older generation of Cromby employees are on view but Dennis is firmly entrenched behind the bar, no doubt fiddling a small fortune for himself. He registers surprise when he sees me.

"Mr. Noggett asked me to mingle and see that everything was under control," I say reassuringly.

"Funny. That's what he told me he was doing." Dennis points across the room and there is Sidney with a large scotch in his hand chatting up a tall bird with butterfly glasses. Dirty old sod! You can't trust anybody these days, can you? He looks up and sees me before I can duck into the crowd and the expression on his mug is not akin to delight. However, he is obviously making headway with the chick because he turns his back and leaves me to it.

"Oh, I am sorry!" The willowy redhead must have made a detour of about five yards to bump into me and is smelling like a fire in a perfume factory that has been put out with liquid supplied by the local brewery.

"That's all right." My smile would make Warren Beatty rush round to his dentist for a check-up. "It was my fault. Let me get you another drink."

"That's very kind of you, but are you sure?"

"What's your pleasure?"

"Now you're asking." She rolls her eyes and gives her pendulum a swing. "Just a teeny gin and tonic. A small one. Really."

Dennis looks up at the ceiling as I approach him and flaps his wrist. "All right for some, isn't it?"

"Keep watering the drinks."

I return to my fair companion who is now chewing her gong temptingly.

"Where's your thing?"

"I beg your pardon!"

"Your pendulum, silly!"

"Oh, that!" I pat my chest absent-mindedly. "Must have left it in my room."

"Did you leave your wife in your room too?"

"She wasn't feeling so well. It must have been someone she ate." She does not seem to find that very funny. Maybe she's right.

"Where are you from?"

"Ur, Clapham." I hesitate because mum has always

103

taught us to say Wandsworth Common because she thinks it sounds better and I am only just breaking myself of the habit.

"Oh, it's lovely, isn't it? We've got lots of friends who have just moved there. The Common is bliss."

I don't know if I would call Scraggs Lane lovely, and when I was a kid the tarts' minders on the common used to keep warm by turning you over for your pocket money. Still, I suppose it has changed a bit in the last few years.

"It's not bad."

"Have you lived there long?"

"Quite a long time, yes." Like all my bleeding life, actually. It is obviously time I changed the subject.

"What's your name?" She holds up her gong and I see that it has Penelope Brown engraved on it.

"Call me Penny. What's yours?"

"Timothy Lea."

"Do you mind being called Tim?"

"I don't mind at all. How's your glass?"

"Fine. I don't think I should have anymore. I'm feeling a bit squiffy as it is. Tell me"—she tugs my sleeve, "are you fixed up yet?" She looks around the assembled swingers and I follow her eyes.

"You mean—?"

"Yes."

"No."

"Well,"—her hand slips into mine and she rests her head against my chest—"how about you and me . . .? I don't want to put the key in." I should think not, it sounds dead uncomfortable. "The last time I ended up with a pervert—there's no other word for it—a pervert who put 'These Boots are Made For Walking' on the record player and started unpacking a pair of Wellingtons. I mean, you can imagine how I felt." I nod sympathetically. "I don't want to have to go through that again."

"No, of course not." I begin to see what she is talking about and my impression is confirmed when Sam the Ram makes with the vocal again.

"Greetings dream-fodder," he murmurs, swaying from

104

ide to side in such a way that his pendulum seems not to be moving. "I'm interrupting the Mellow Mingle because it is time for the Ceremony of the Keys. Gather round, those of you with a burning yearning for nude feels and postures new."

"He's so cool," breathes Penny.

"Who, Sam?"

"*Big* Sam," she gives an ecstatic little wriggle and I wince. "Come on, I want to watch this."

We press forward to where a circle has formed in front of the Ram and what looks like a black velvet pillow case is lying on the ground. About twenty birds step forward and put their rooms keys into the bag and there is a feeling of excitement in the air. Quite a lot of straightforward feeling too.

"Everybody done? Then let's start swinging!" Big S. whirls the bag about his head and a bunch of blokes press forward when he stops. Like kids with a lucky dip, they dive their hands into the bag and draw out a key. "Forty-seven", "twenty-eight", "sixty-nine"—that one gets a laugh. As the numbers are called out so the blokes pair off with the bird whose room key they have got. All except one man whose voice rises in cheated outrage:

"Oih!" he shouts, "I've got my wife." The unhappy accident is quickly remedied and couples drift back to the bar and off to amuse each other. Disgusting, isn't it? Yeah, but a bit of all right as well, eh? I wonder what my mum and dad would have been like if they had gone in for this caper? They could not have been much worse off. I will wager that.

"I didn't think much of Christopher's," says Penny as she takes my arm.

"Christopher's what—oh, you mean his bird." I don't really want to know which one is Christopher. I am old fashioned like that. If I am knocking off the missus I don't fancy a game of darts with hubby afterwards. I am more interested in seeing what has happened to Sid. Oh, dear! Sam the Ram is leading off Butterfly Specs, and Sid is looking like a kid who hid his lolly ice in a warm oven. I consider issuing a few words of good cheer, but decide against it. Sid can turn a bit funny sometimes. With this thought in mind I quicken my pace as we leave the ballroom, and study the key that Penny has thoughtfully pushed into my mitt.

"It's fantastic to meet someone new," she murmurs. "You get tired of all the old faces."

At the very least, I think to myself. Blimey, how many couples in the hotel? Two hundred? She should write a book about it. Perhaps she has.

We pad along the corridor and there it is. Room number one-eight-two. I take a deep breath as I unlock it because I have a nasty feeling that Christopher is going to be on the other side with a shot gun. Sometimes I think I belong to another age. Every time I get my end away I think I am doing something naughty. Does make it more exciting though.

"Nobody here," I say, my voice sounding a bit strained

"Of course not, darling. You weren't expecting a gangers, were you?"

"A what?"

"Gangers bangers, darling."

"Oh, yes. Of course not."

"Tomorrow night. Now, that's another story. You weren't with us at Bournemouth were you? We united with a working sub-committee of the British Foundrymen's Association —and I mean united."

"Sounds a great scene," I say, trying to appear as if I experience it every day of the week before the Epilogue. "Christopher won't come barging in will he?"

"Good heavens, no. We won't see him till kipper-time We have eight hours to amuse each other." She sways towards me and I wonder if eight hours is going to be long enough. I have always been partial to a bit of tit myself and this bird is not particularly well favoured in that direction, but she has a slinky quality that more than makes up for it. Her body ripples like a flag in a hurricane and she plants herself against my body like she is trying to turn herself into a laminate. I push the door shut with my foot

106

and immediately feel able to deal with the situation. At least I think I do. I allow Penny the access to my lips she so obviously demands and rub my hands gently over her curvy hind-quarters. No need to hurry things. Mrs. Brown has other ideas. Her fingernails dig into me like she is probing for a 50p. piece that has slipped down the lining of my jacket and her mouth performs as if it is trying to douse a forest fire. "Come on, oh no, baby! Please! No, yes. Oh—o-o-o-h!!! Do it to me. Please! Ple-e-e-ase!!!' Well, you don't have to be a boy scout to respond to a plea like that and I set to unzipping her like a starving cannibal welcoming a new missionary. Her own hands are not idle and her assault on the front of my trousers would qualify for the finals of the World Turnip-Picking Championships. Once again, I wish I had the services of Ejecta pants as I try and struggle free from the clinging embrace of my jealous underwear. These fits of passion can be murder on a young trendy's wardrobe for the modern satins and velvets are not well-equipped for displays of sexual violence. Sit down a bit sudden and you could rip the seat out of seven quids worth of flare-bottomed invitation to sensual mayhem. Get down to a real bit of sweaty slap and tickle and you might as well resign yourself to five quids worth of invisible mending or a quick conversion to faded denim.

"Gr-r-r-h!" Mrs. B. is now making growling noises. Her bra and panties set is really something. Midnight blue with little red flowers scattered everywhere. You can see she has chosen her wardrobe with real care. I am now naked except for my socks and so look like a refugee from a dirty photograph. I always feel a right berk in this condition and attempt to cater for Mrs. B.'s increasingly excited demands while hopping from one leg to another trying to hook off my Wolsey grip-tops. Only a mountain goat—and I have seen very few of them about tonight—could achieve the necessary standard of footwork and it is seconds before I crash back across the bed with Penny on top of me. Luckily my equipment is wangy enough to withstand the impact and I lie back as my excitable friend struggles to her feet and whips off her bra and panties.

"Don't move Lancelot," she yodels, giving a long ecstatic wriggle that makes me think she is trying to shed her skin. "That's just the way I want you." I have no pláns to cross-index my stamp collection, so I continue to lie back and wait for her to vault into the saddle. But not a bit of it.

While I watch in amazement she gets a large cardboard box and starts emptying some white powder into the washbasin. What is this? Is she going to rinse out her smalls or is it some kind of Ajax demonstration? Is a fast-talker with a microphone and forty-two Birmingham housewives going to appear from behind the curtains?

"I'm going to add you to my collection," she says, turning on the cold tap. "Did you see 'W.R. Mysteries of the Orgasm'?"

"No!" I say indignantly. I mean, it does not sound very nice does it? What is she on about?

"You should do. It's a marvellous movie." She is clearly mixing something in the washbasin. What is it? Bread? She wipes her hands on a towel and comes over to the bed.

"Now," she says gently, "let's get him ready." She sits down on the edge of the bed and starts running her fingers gently along my hampton. My friend laps this up and I stretch out my finger to perform a similar service.

"Later," she murmurs, crossing one leg over the other, "let me do this first." It occurs to me that her tone has changed a bit from the first moments of careless rapture—and near rupture, and that her efforts were directed towards achieving the fine specimen her fingers are now feasting on. I do not like being manipulated in this way, but on the other hand—or perhaps in the other hand—I do, if you know what I mean.

"Like a sword isn't it?" she observes cheerfully. "Now, just a little—" Her mouth drops and I have to hold onto the edge of the bed. Oh, my goodness me! All part of life's rich varied tapestry, as my old school master used to say—though not about what Mrs. Brown is doing to me. There must be worse ways of spending Friday night.

"Right," says Mrs. B. climbing to her feet. "He's ready." She can say that again. You could fire my hampton through the side of a Centurion tank without denting it. "No, don't move."

Before I can grab her she has nipped over to the washbasin and return with two handfuls of white gunge which she slaps on top of my throbbing J.T.! Talk about surprised! I am speechless.

"Hey! What the—"

"Plaster of paris, Lancelot. I'm taking a cast of your virility." She slaps some more gunk over puzzled Percy and smiles down at me. "It won't take a second. This stuff dries very fast."

"But, why? What are you going to use it for?"

"Just a souvenir. I'm not going to turn it into a dildo. Though that's quite a good idea, isn't it? Dildos of the famous. You could sign up all the sexiest showbiz personalities and even royalty. Comfort yourself with the Duke of—"

"Hold on a minute," I croak. "Are you sure this isn't going to damage my equipment?"

"Darlingest, would I perform such a disservice to my baser interests?" She squeezes the plaster of Paris tightly round my hampton and kisses me lightly on the lips. "I'll send you one if you like. You can use it as a paper weight."

"Thanks. My mum would like that."

"You don't have to show it to her. I keep my collection in the bureau."

The bureau of missing persons, I think to myself. Blimey. What a carry on. There are a lot of funny people about, aren't there?"

"It's hardened up nicely," she says. "Now, where's my hammer?"

"Good evening!" Those of you who have ever tried to leap off a bed with half a pound of plaster of paris round your chopper will sympathise with my predicament.

"Don't be silly," she says. "It's only a little tap."

"I know, but I've grown fond of it over the years."

"I mean it's only a little tap with the hammer. You won't feel a thing."

"That's what my dentist used to say."

109

She produces a small hammer, like the ones you get in a kid's carpentry set and advances towards the bed.

"You'd better know what you're doing with that thing."

"Darling, it's easy as breaking an egg." My balls don't go for that much I can tell you. Tap, tap. "There you are." I make a "let's wait and see" noise and watch my happy hampton burst out into the light again like a friendly moggy that has been locked up in a dark room. Mrs. B. takes the two halves of the cast and puts them together carefully.

"I'll deal with these later," she says, popping them into the top drawers of the dressing table.

"Yeah, now you can start dealing with this." I grab her by the arm and yank her onto the bed.

"Darling, I really ought to put something on it first."

"I'll tell you what to put on it!" I am not interested in garnish. I am interested in action. I have waited a long time and my equipment has been sorely mis-used. "Come on top of me." Mrs. B. straddles me on her knees and I plunge Percy into darkness again—this time in surroundings to which he is more accustomed. "Come here." I am not usually rough with ladies but at this moment I need a little agro to rekindle my lapsed enthusiasm. I pull Penny down so that her breasts rub against my chest and her hair tickles my cheeks. I brush it aside and feast on her mouth stroking her cheeks as if coaxing out her tongue from a hiding place. Her body begins to rise and fall across my hips and I time the flexing of my muscles to coincide with hers. Beautiful! And such good exercise too. I am certain this must be better for you than all those bloody stupid exercises they print in women's magazines.

"Put your knees up," she says, "I want to lean back." I let her go and watch the expression on her face as she settles herself in the position to achieve maximum satisfaction. Her eyes are half-closed and she breathes in little pockets of air almost as if she is in pain. Slowly her tongue extends to be held gingerly between her teeth and her mouth broadens into the beginnings of a smile.

"Go on," she whispers, "go on, go on!" Pressing her hands down against the bed she pushes her body up and down in time with the flexing of my hips. "Oh, darling, that's heaven." I read somewhere—I don't think it was in the Women's Institute Year Book—that birds have been known to faint with ecstasy in such a position. I don't blame them. I am feeling a bit giddy myself.

"Oh! Oh! Oh!" Is it her or me calling out? I close my eyes and open my mouth and what happens after that is Ike and Tina Turner destroying the volume control on the greatest stereo set on earth. That and some miserable old git banging on the ceiling with an artificial limb. You can't please everybody I suppose.

I don't know what the time is when we eventually get to sleep but I feel as though I have been run through a combine harvester a couple of times. Talk about knackered! I close my eyes and when I open them the sunlight is streaming through the windows. Blimey! I should be somewhere else fast. I leap out of bed and land on something soft. Something soft that groans. It is a man stretched out on the bedside rug.

"Sorry," says the creature, still half asleep but sounding genuinely apologetic. "I couldn't stand the woman's snoring." I presume he means the bird he was shacked up with. This must be Christopher. I don't wait to introduce myself but pull on my trousers and leave him clambering wearily into bed to take my place beside Mrs. B. who is still out for the count.

So endeth the first night that the Pendulum Society spend at the Cromby. It is a taste of things to come.

CHAPTER SEVEN

As luck would have it, Sidney is standing just inside the dining room as I try and sneak to my place and the expression on his face could not be interpreted as welcoming even by an Icelandic Trade Delegation.

"Where have you been?" he says.

"You wouldn't believe me if I told you," I say, trying to swallow a yawn.

"You look bloody awful."

"I got a bit plastered last night," I say wittily.

"Well, you'd better get on with it. I'll talk to you later."

"Yes Sidney."

I am hoping that Christopher and Penny will be too knackered to come down to breakfast but, of course, they are the first couple I see, staring at their packet of Rice Crispies as if it has the meaning of life scrawled on the back.

"Morning!" I say brightly. Mrs. Brown's face registers surprise but this is soon replaced by an expression not far distant from outrage.

"You're a waiter!" she says.

"That's right." I could explain that I stand on the right hand side of Sid the All-nighty, but what is the point?

"You're not one of us?"

"An imposter."

"How dare you! You took advantage of me."

"Get stuffed." The last words are mine. I mean, it's a bit much isn't it? Ruthlessly exploited all night and then rejected because my credentials do not come up to par. How middle class. I wonder she did not ask for a blood sample.

My little outburst raises a few eyebrows around us but most of these are drooping like they have lead weights sewed at the corners. The night was obviously one of non-stop pelvic-bashing. I change tables with one of the other waiters and leave the Browns to splutter over their kipper fillets. My cock-cast is never going to see the inside of Mrs. B.'s bureau. Too bad. I was thinking there might be a few bob in flogging them as alternatives to garden gnomes.

Out in the vestibule a sign directs club members to an address by one Professor Mordecai Hucklejohn entitled "Marriage—Whither or Wither?" and quite a few of them troop into the ballroom after breakfast. They must regret it because no sooner has Professor Hucklejohn asked for a glass of iced water than a gang of micks roll up and start tearing down the building next door. They have obviously been concentrating on the Liffywater or given orders to make as much noise as possible because the Prof's instructive words are soon drowned by the din of falling masonry and language that would make a Billingsgate fish porter blush. Added to that clouds of dust drift in through every window in the place. Rigby's war has begun.

"It's a bugger, isn't it?" says Sid, "but there's nothing I can do about it, short of dumping him out to sea with a weighing machine tied to his ankles. I've been to the Town Hall but, like he said, they don't want to know. We'll just have to plough on regardless. I'm not giving in."

"Has he been in touch with you?"

"Yes, he rang up last night. Cocky bastard. I told him what he could do with himself. Oh dear, here comes trouble." He refers to Sam the Ram who is approaching shaking his head ruefully.

"Nobody can hear a word in there, man," he says. "How long before they start on this place and we can all go home?"

"I'm very sorry about that, Sir, but I am afraid the whole situation is caused by circumstances beyond my control—" Sid sounds as if he is reading a bulletin fixed to the gates of Buckingham Palace, but my thoughts are elsewhere. Supposing Riley's mob did start trying to knock down the Cromby? That could well spark off enough scandal to force weasel-features to halt his dastardly plans for a bit.

I potter about until lunch-time and then pop round to the local boozer. As anticipated the sons of Eire are tucking into a well-earned glass of lunch and I salute them cheerfully.

"Hello there, me boyos," I chant, trying to get a lilt into my voice, "the top of the morning to you. And a fine day it is for a drop of the hard stuff."

"Bugger off!"

Attempts to get alongside these lusty lads are obviously going to have to be handled with a bit more subtlety.

"Sure, and I'm having the divil's own trouble with this dratted crossword," I continue. "Could you be tickling my memory with the information as to the longest river in the dear old Emerald Isle?"

"I'll be tickling your back passage with the toe of my boot if you don't fuck off!" Unpleasantly dirty fingers close round my throat and I get a Cinerama Holiday view of half a dozen blackened stumps which might just once have been teeth. The owner of this gross affront to the British Dental Association sprays my mug with saliva and a whiff of rotting vegetation which could be used to gas rats. "We've had enough of youse perverts," he continues, moving my head around with his hand as if trying to find a crack in the wall which might fit it. "If you don't get your backside out of this bar in the next two minutes, you'll get my drill up it."

"Don't encourage him to stay, Paddy," says a large gentleman with a face like a plate-full of boiled potatoes, "to his kind that's a promise, not a threat."

"Throw him out!"

"Murder him!"

"Papist!"

It occurs to me, as my backside collides with the pavement, that this is one plan which I can forget about in a big way. I had formed a hazy idea of getting the micks so pissed that they would find it difficult to tell the difference between the Cromby, the apartment house next door, and a set of kids building bricks. With them swinging their big lead ball against the dining room windows, it might have been possible to alert the local press to another example of property developing vandalism. No such luck. Not content with inflicting injury on my precious person the surly sons of the sod are back after dinner bashing away twice as hard—but with no loss of accuracy. The building next door is falling apart before my eyes and the Cromby remains dusty but intact.

Awareness of the life-style of the Pendulum Society has not been slow to sweep through the ranks of the Cromby staff.

"When I brought in the tea they asked for two extra cups," says June primly. "They were lined up across the bed."

"Four of them?" says Carmen.

"No, six. Two of them only drank coffee."

"There's decadent for you," I say. "You sound as if you don't approve?"

"It's not very nice, is it?" drones Carmen.

"How can you ravers have the gall to say that?" I scold them. "You've never been fussed about hunting as a pack."

"But we're not married," says Audrey reproachfully. "It's different for them. They shouldn't behave like that."

"It's not nice," repeats Carmen.

"You mean to tell me that when you get married you're never going to have a bit on the side?"

"No!"

"The very idea!"

"I should think not!"

Amazing isn't it? The ways of women never cease to amaze me. Take my sister, Rosie, for instance. There was a time when everybody used to. Yours for a tanners' worth of chips and first shake with the vinegar bottle, they used to say around us. She got married to Sidney—very sudden it was—and after that butter would not melt between her thighs. The perfect wife and mother—until she gets a whiff of Ricci Volare. Then, pow! Right back to square one, or round one would be more appropriate. How she is going to react to the Pendulum Society I will be interested to find out. If I was Sid I would not be viewing her impending visit with enthusiasm. It is about half past four when the family arrive and dad's reaction is typical.

"Hello," he says, "pulling it down already are they? Vermin, is it?"

"It's the place next door, dad."

"Building an extension already, is he?" says mum, the super optimist.

"Not yet mum, though we're pretty full at the moment."

"Nice class of person," says mum, gazing admiringly at one of the Pendulum lot who is walking a poodle in a dramatic trouser suit—she has the trouser suit, not the poodle.

"Yeah. What do you think, Rosie?" But Rosie is gazing at Sam the Ram who flashes his evil lust-laden eyes at her as he brushes past her looking as if he has got about one and a half foot of fire hose down the front of his trousers. Her expression is one I remember uncomfortably from the Isla de Amor: Rosie wants it. Really, one's relations can be a terrible embarrassment sometimes. I said, "Jason has just stubbed his icecream out in your handbag, Rosie." That brings her round a bit sudden, and by the time little J., who looks more like his revolting father every day, gets past the reception area in a flood of tears, I reckon her mind may be on other things.

I hope it is, because Sidney chooses that moment to roll up, picking burrs out of his turn-ups. He has obviously been taking a spot of physical exercise with Sandra who wanders by a discreet few moments later looking redder than my mum when she mistook the gents at Clapham Common for the entrance to the tube station. Sid, himself, is looking a bit flustered which mum chooses to interpret as a sign of work strain. Now that mum reckons Sid is worth a few bob he can do no wrong, while with dad acute dislike has grown into seething hatred.

"You haven't been overdoing it, I hope, dear?" says mum. Sid avoids my eyes and smacks a couple of kisses on the Lea ladies.

"No fear of that, mum, you know me. Hello Rosie love. I didn't expect you so early. Hello Jason!!" Sid pops on his "I love kids" expression but it does not cut any ice with little Lord Nausea.

"S'cream! S'cream! S'cream!" he wails. "I wanna s'cream, wanna s'cream."

"But he is screaming," says Sid, perplexed.

"He wants an ice cream, you berk," I tell him. "Blimey, Sid, can't you even understand your own kid?"

"He never sees him long enough to be able to recognise him properly," says Rosie. "I tell you, if he saw him

116

walking down the other side of the street he wouldn't recognise him."

"Oh yes I would," says Sid, all indignant. "He'd be the one dressed like a two-year-old poufdah."

It is true that Rosie's tastes do veer a little towards the Carnaby in toddler's wear and I would not like to be left at nursery school in some of the clobber he gets landed with unless I had a flick knife hidden under my rompers. Nevertheless, Rosie is sensitive on the point.

"I want the child to look nice, that's all. If it was left to you, he'd still be wearing that thing they gave him at the hospital."

"He'll be on the turn soon. You mark my words, that's how they all start. If you want a girl let's have another one. Don't try and make him ambidextrous."

"Fine chance of that when we don't even live together, isn't there?"

All through this fairly typical Lea family reunion, Jason's screams are getting louder and louder and it is perhaps fortunate that Miss Ruperts arrives on the scene to restore a little queenly decorum. She appears to be very good with children and my mum, and takes them off for a cup of tea, a liquid which could float ma through a martian invasion.

"She is in one of her moods, I can tell that," says Sid, when Rosie has been led away to the Bridal Suite. "She can be very funny sometimes."

He does not say any more, but I have a feeling that some sixth sense, or sexth sinse, is carrying his mind back to the Ricci Volare episode on one of Spain's unsettled colonies. He never actually caught them on the job, but I think he suspected more than he rationalised, if you know what I mean.

It is just as well that he is not with me when Rosie comes back from the beach an hour later. She has taken Jason down for a paddle and, I reckon, as an excuse to get into her new multi-piece bathing costume. The one in which none of the pieces quite covers the bit it is supposed to be covering.

117

"Ooh, he is nice," she says.

"Who?"

"That big fellow, Sam something. He had a bottle of spirit down the front of his trunks—" I feel better already. "—got all the oil off Jason's legs. It's disgraceful isn't it. Sidney should complain to somebody."

"He can't find Liberia on the map."

"No? Well, this fellow was so kind. He was marvellous with Jason. He asked me if I was going to the dance tonight."

"No!" Maybe the words did come out a bit quick.

"What do you mean 'no'. It's in the hotel isn't it. I'm the owner's wife."

"Yeah, but it's private."

"Not if I've been invited by the President of the Society. That's what he said he was."

"I don't want her going anywhere near there! It's disgusting!" Sidney's reaction when I tell him of Rosie's plans is not totally unexpected.

"But you went, Sidney," I say innocently.

"Don't push your luck, it's different for fellers. Everybody knows that. Anyway, nothing happened."

"Only because your bird went off with that big bloke. He's the one that invited Rosie to the dance." I get more satisfaction out of Sid's face than from an old Laurel and Hardy movie.

"I don't want to see her there," he says, gulping. "You know what she's like. Give her a few drinks and she loses control. The wrong kind of bloke could take advantage of her."

"I always wondered how you two came to be married."

"That's enough of that. I'm serious. I've got a position to uphold here and I don't want any embarrassment. It's in your interest too, you know. She's your sister."

"What do you expect me to do about it?"

"There's a show down on the Pier, 'Frisky Follies of 1902' or something. I'll get some tickets and you can take them off there."

"Take what off there?"

118

"Oh, blimey. Take mum, dad and Rosie off there of course. That should keep them out of harm's way."

"What about you?"

"I'll have to stay here, won't I? After all I am the owner."

"But I like dancing."

"No you don't. You like getting your end away. Tonight you'll have to do without it. Your job is to keep Rosie away from that dance floor."

"But, Sid—"

"No 'buts'. You let me down on this one and you'll be able to flog your old man for valve washers."

Sid can come on a bit heavy with the old-world charm sometimes and at such moments it is unwise to push the agrochat. I swallow back my resentment and prepare for the tedium ahead. Hoverton's light entertainment industry is no threat to Broadway and seeing any show with my parents has been a source of embarrassment since they took me to a pantomime at Clapham Junction. First of all they always sit on somebody else's lap and then dad finds a seat and sits on it while it is still tipped up. He wonders why everybody is shouting at him and a right old how's your father goes on until the manager and three usherettes force him into a seat like a ventriloquist's dummy. Then he never understands what is happening.

"Why is he doing that, mother?" he demands. "Look, look, they've got it wrong. He's got different clothes on."

Perhaps dad's worst fault is that he has always seen everything. Despite only having been to the flicks about six times in his life, there is always one moment in every film when he suddenly springs to his feet, points at the screen and exclaims, "I've seen it, I've seen it. The bloke with the 'tash does it." He even did that in the "Sound of Music".

Perhaps he will be better at the live theatre. He is always rambling on about how you could not beat the old music hall.

Rosie is definitely not pleased at the evening that has been arranged for her.

"I don't want to go down the pier," she says as she

shovels in her last mouthful of fruit salad. "Is Sid ashamed of us or something?"

"I think it's 'or something'" I murmur under my breath. "Come on, Rosie, cheer up! I've heard it's a great show."

"Who's in it then?" I rack my brain for some of the half-forgotten names of yesteryear.

"Terry Grimley—"

"He's not still alive is he," says dad, wiping the custard off his chin—some of it anyway. "I remember him when I was a boy."

"Radio's 'Mr. Romance'," I continue lamely.

"I wouldn't cross the street to see him wrestling in mud with Donald Peers," snorts Rosie.

"Then there's the Amazing Arturo."

"What's amazing about him?"

"I don't know. He juggles I think."

"Big deal."

"And Renato and his Little Squeaking Friends."

"Is that the one who has the vampire bats that feed him sugar lumps? Oh, I've seen that on the tele." Mum is obviously impressed.

"It sounds disgusting to me," sniffs Rosie. "I don't want to go."

"Have a cherry brandy," I say, waving desperately for a waiter. In fact, Rosie has three cherry brandys before I deem her sufficiently mellow to be led off to the Pier Pavilion. With maximum cunning I steer the conversation round to the brilliance of little Jason, always a subject calculated to soothe her savage breasts.

I have hopes of escaping from the hotel before the Pendulum Swingers finish dusting the inside of their toes with talcum powder but this is not to be. As we pass the ballroom, Sam the Ram is having words with the hotel electrician.

"All those lights we can do without," he says. "I'm not planning to conduct an autopsy in there. Let's make it strictly fanny by gaslight, you dig?"

"We'd better hurry along," I say, glancing at my watch, but it is no good. Rosie gives the kind of delicate little cough which has been known to spark off avalanches and lurches into King Conk.

"Oh!" she says, "it's you."

"You're absolutely right," he says. "Geeze, but you're looking lovely." When he turns round I can see that he is wearing a white ruffled shirt open at the neck and his trousers are so tight they look as if they have leaked through his pores. "I hope you're going to save me a dance tonight?"

"I'm being taken to the theatre," says Rosie, making it sound like she means quarantine centre.

"Come along later." Sam smiles and runs his hand lightly up her arm. "I'd love to get you on the dance floor." The way he looks at her you know he means any floor. This bloke is definitely another Ricci Volare.

"Charming, wasn't he?" says mum, when I have eventually dragged Rosie away.

"He looked a great pouf if you ask me," says dad, speaking the truth for once. "What's he want to go wearing a woman's blouse for?"

"Oh dad, don't be so stupid. It's fashionable to wear shirts like that."

"He won't do himself any good in those trousers either. The body has got to breathe."

"In your case. I wonder why sometimes."

"Now, that's unkind, Rosie."

"Typical, bleeding typical—"

"—He shouldn't go on like that—"

"—Slave your fingers to the bone to give your kids a decent start in life and—"

"Belt up, both of you," I groan. "Let's get to the bleeding pier before it closes down for the winter."

"No need for coarse language, dear," says mum. "I've noticed you've been a lot more free in your speech since you went on that boat." Mum has a very low opinion of sailors, especially those not blessed by the sight of the Red Ensign fluttering at the masthead. I imagine it stems from an unhappy incident in her youth.

121

"It was a very coarsening experience, mother," I tell her. Little does she know.

Rosie is still sulking when we get to the pier. Maybe this has something to do with the fact that it has been raining since we left the hotel and I have been unable to find a cab.

"This pair of shoes are ruined," she moans.

"Oh, they're shoes are they," says dad. "I thought you'd forgotten to take them out of their box."

"They've got cork soles dad, it's fashionable."

"Bloody handy if it rains anymore. You can float home."

"You sure we've got the right night?" says mum, "there don't seem to be many people here."

"I'm not surprised," sniffs Rosie. "Terry Grimley. Oh, my gawd."

When we get onto the pier the planks are glistening with rain and the coloured bulbs—those that have not been broken—swinging in the gusty wind.

"I think I'll walk off the end of the pier and drown myself like Necrophilia," says Rosie.

"You mean Ophelia, don't you?" I tell her. Rosie has a big thing for Richard Chamberlain and ever since seeing him as Hamlet on the tele, has liked to crash in with the odd Shakespearean reference. Very odd, some of them.

"Alright, clever-shanks," she snaps, "have it your way."

Boy, this is going to be a marvellous evening, I think to myself as I slap down the complimentary tickets. I have not stood such a good chance of enjoying myself since we ran out of candles during the power strike.

Inside the theatre there are less people than at a meeting of Jack the Ripper's fan club and Rosie starts moaning again before I have bought the programmes.

"I can't stand it," she says. "I just can't stand it."

"Oh, look," says mum, "what a shame—Terry Grimley is 'indisposed'."

"Thank God," says Rosie nastily.

"Still, there's always 'Renato and his Little Squeaking Friends' mum," I say cheerfully. How right I am!

The orchestra sound as if they were introduced to each other five minutes before they started playing the National

Anthem and the opening number, "Hoverton, Hoverton, It's not a Bovver-town!"—at least I think that is what they are singing—could be one of the most forgettable tunes written in the last twenty years. The chorus girls look like rotarians in drag and their make-up could have been put on by a bloke responsible for painting puppets. All in all, the production lives down to my worst fears and I dare not look at Rosie.

The opening number gives way—maybe, surrenders, would be a better word—to one of the lousiest ventriloquists I have ever seen. The patter is so bad that the dummy must have written it and the ventriloquist moves his lips more than a short-sighted lodger trying to spit out his landlady's dentures. After that comes a Scottish comedian who does imitations of Andy Stewart doing imitations of Harry Lauder, and two child tap dancers who make up in clumsiness what they lack in skill.

"How much longer to the interval," whispers Rosie. "I can't take much more."

"After the bats," I tell her. "They're on next." She shudders and I sit back as a decrepit looking geezer wearing a black cloak and false eye teeth—at least, I imagine they are false—comes out onto the stage and spreads his arms wide to receive the non-existent applause. He waits hopefully for a few seconds and then waves a hand towards the wings. From the other side of the stage one of the chorus girls teeters out holding a large cage at arm's length. I can sympathise with her distaste because when Renato whips off the cover I can see what appears to be half a dozen broken black umbrellas hanging in an ugly cluster. My reaction is not an isolated one because a combined exclamation of disgust is the biggest noise produced by the audience the whole evening.

"Ooh! I don't fancy that!" says Rosie.

"Imagine one of those in your hair," says mum. I remember her words later.

The chorus girl gingerly inserts her hand into the cage and then withdraws it sharply.

"It bit her," gasps mum.

123

"I'm getting out," says Rosie.

"Don't be daft," says dad. "They're just trying to build up the suspense. I remember once, at the Finsbury Empire—"

"Shut up, dad."

Renato moves forward swiftly and elbows his unfortunate assistant aside before plunging his mitt into the cage. More kerfuffle and one of the bats is drawn into the open. The audience sucks in its breath. Renato holds up the bat and produces what appears to be a lump of sugar from inside his robe. His miserable assistant is made to hold the bat by the tip of its wings and Renato advances to the footlights. Like a kid showing off the first tooth it loses, he flashes the sugar at the audience between finger and thumb and places it between his lips. The girl gratefully releases the bat which circles a couple of times and then swoops down to alight on the area of Renato's mouth.

"I'm going to be sick," says Rosie.

The sugar disappears and the bat takes off and zooms into the wings. I do not think it should do this unless Renato gets through an awful lot of bats in his act. Certainly, the Maestro's face clouds over for a second as he gazes after his little squeaking friend.

"He swallowed it," says dad firmly.

"Don't be silly, dear. It flew off the stage."

"Not the bat, you stupid old bag. The piece of sugar."

"I'm going to be sick," says Rosie.

"There it is," says mum.

High above our heads the errant bat is circling the theatre, presumably looking for some means of getting out. I know just how it feels.

"I hope it hasn't been fed recently," says mum.

"Do you mind!" says dad. "That kind of talk isn't nice."

"Having your hair messed up isn't nice either," scolds mum. "I had this done special." There is no doubt that mum's bonce does resemble petrified meringue.

"Oh, no!" breathes Rosie. "What's he going to do now?"

Renato is filling his cake-hole with lumps of sugar and the beginnings of a drum roll tell us that the act is approaching its climax. The unwilling assistant takes the remaining bats across the stage in their cage and Renato advances to the footlights.

"I don't want to watch," Rosie buries her face in her hands. I glance at mum whose eyes are wider than serving hatches. Dad is looking up at the ceiling. This kind of thing is probably very old hat after the Finsbury Empire. The drum roll reaches a crescendo and the girl on the stage gingerly releases the catch on the cage and withdraws her hand swiftly. Nothing happens. She waits for a moment and gives the cage a shake. Still nothing happens. Beginning to panic she turns the cage on its side and shakes it viciously until, like sticky pastry, the bats begin to peel away.

After that things happen fast. A stream of bats make for Renato while one stays behind to menace his assistant. She screams, drops the cage and runs from the stage. Maybe this upsets the rest of the bats. They descend on Renato's cake-hole like wasps on a squashed plum. There is an exclamation of pain that carries beyond the back row of the upper circle and Renato reels sideways, clapping his hand to his mouth and spraying the first three rows of the stalls with lumps of sugar. Obviously one of his little friends has taken the dead needle with him.

The bats swoop down into the audience like low flying aircraft and the next thing I know, mum has one in her hair. I have heard some noises in my time but the sounds coming from mum cap everything.

"Ooooeeeooww!!!" she shrieks. "Get it out! Get it out!" The bat is squeaking and flapping away fit to burst and I see its evil little rat face and those teeth. Teeth! By the cringe, they are like something out of a horror comic. Around us the audience is in uproar and Renato is jumping off the edge of the stage. I tear my jacket off and throw it over mum's head. I have no intention of touching the bat with my bare hands. I close my hands around the disgusting quivering body—the bat's I mean—and consider squeezing the life out of it. I don't have to make the decision because Renato pushes me aside and whips off the jacket.

"You are a madman!?" he hisses. "You want to destroy me my little friend. See? She is frightened."

"What about my old woman?" explodes dad. "She's just had her bleeding hair done. This lot is going to set you back a few bob."

Renato ignores him.

"Come, come Bettina," he soothes, "your pappa is here to look after you." Mum's screams must now be jamming local radio stations. They are certainly not doing anything to calm down Bettina who sinks her treacherous fangs into Renato's thumb as he extends a rescuing hand.

"Aagh!!" The Maestro staggers back and a row of seats collapses taking mum and dad with it. In the confusion Bettina tears herself free and zooms off to join her little chums aloft. Dad belts Senor Renato up the bracket and Rosie disappears.

The last event is in many ways the most disturbing but I do not notice it until we have steered mum into the Manager's office and started getting her outside a bottle of brandy. The show has been abandoned and Senor Renato is standing in the deserted auditorium trying to talk down his little friends who are sulking amongst the rafters. Dad is beside himself with ecstasy having never actually connected with a blow before in his life.

"He should never have tried it on with me," he says. "He was a fool to himself. He should never have done it. I showed him, didn't I, love? I wasn't going to have that Eyetie making you cry and getting away with it."

"You caught him in the mouth with your elbow when he turned round a bit sharpish," says mum. "When he fell down you hit him again. Now do belt up about it. All I want to do is get away from here."

It is then that I notice that Rosie has beaten her to it. Leaving mum with her hand comfortably anchored to the neck of the brandy bottle and dad trying to explain to the manager that free seats for the next performance are something short of adequate reparation for the mental and physical anguish caused, I race out into the still-rainy night just in time to reach the turnstile as Rosie is climbing into a taxi.

I shout at her but she chooses not to hear and the taxi draws away. Knickers! Sidney is going to do his nut.

I waste valuable time hanging around for another taxi and then start running along the promenade. Every shelter is either full of tramps dossing down for the night or couples groping each other. These tableaux of fumbling lust sharpen my mind to thoughts of what is happening back at the Cromby. Will I get there in time to prevent Rosie tangling with Sam the Ram? Will Sidney be exposed in mid-grapple with some sexed-up swinger? New readers begin here.

I charge through the doors of the Cromby and run straight into Miss Primstone who is standing by the reception looking as enthusiastic as a bloodhound that has just received an estimate for a face lift.

"Have you seen Mrs. Noggett?" I pant. Miss Primstone sighs.

"I believe you will find her in the ballroom." It is the way that she shudders on the word "ballroom" that terrifies me.

"And Mr. Noggett?"

"I believe the little boy was having teething problems, Mr. Noggett is tending him upstairs."

"Good." Miss Primstone's eyebrows rise. "I mean I'm glad Sidney is looking after him."

Maybe there is still time. I move with Elliot Ness swiftness to the ballroom expecting to hear orgy-type noises assaulting my ear drums. To my surprise there is only the subdued throb of music beating with a heart-like regularity. I open the door and it takes my eyes a few seconds to get used to the darkness. The whole of one wall is a gigantic screen onto which have been projected patterns and images which move slowly like drops of coloured water finding a path through packed ice. As I follow them down to floor level I become aware of shadowy shapes, glistening limbs, heaps of discarded clothing. Blimey! I am too late.

Or am I? About the only couple performing in a vertical plane are Sam and Rosie. He is holding her to him like she is a rolled-up carpet he is transporting down a steep flight of stairs but as far as I can make out they still have their clobber on. How long this very desirable state of affairs is going to last is another matter. Sam's pelvic region is revolving like one of those attachments available with a Black and Decker kit and Rosie is one stage away from total knicker-loss. Alack, alas, what can I do? Any second now Sidney will return from providing succour to his fledgling Noggett and Rosie's 36A cup is not going to be the only thing that is undone. If only she was not so impetuous! Still, I suppose it runs in the family.

"Having a nice time, aren't they?" I turn round and craggy Petheridge is at my elbow. "I thought I was a bit of a raver but this lot leave me standing. You'd need to turn on the sprinkler system to separate them, wouldn't you?"

"What?!" I say, a giant "thinks" bubble bursting from my nut.

"I said you'd need to turn on the sprinkler system to separate them."

"Oh, yeah." I try and sound dead casual. "You mean down the end of the corridor on the third floor?"

"Yes. Hey, look at those two! They're going at it aren't they?"

Experienced readers will have no difficulty in knowing which two he is talking about, and my feet develop wings as I speed towards the third floor. I am belting down the long corridor when a door opens and—surprise, surprise— I am face to face with Sidney Noggett. His face is flushed and it does not look as if this is due to the strain of ministering to little Jason. I obtain this impression from the sight of the buxom red head who is patting her hair into place beside the crumpled bed.

"Where's Rosie?" yelps Sidney, his voice combining both fear and menace.

"She's on her way," I shout over my shoulder, I reckon this being a fairly accurate statement of the situation. Sidney says something else but I don't hear him because I am round the corner and flinging open the door marked "no admittance".

The inside of the room resembles the control room of

a Victorian Cape Kennedy. Brass switches and cobweb-covered circuits abound and I look desperately for some instructions. In my panic I press a large switch and realise that it is not the right one when the light in the room goes out. Ah! There we are! "Sprinkler System". "Foyer", "dining room", "ballroom". I take a deep breath and pull the lever as far as it will go. I hope to God that Sidney has not got to the ballroom yet. To add to my good fortune there is a key on the inside of the lock. I grab it, hop out into the corridor and lock the door behind me. That should keep everybody off their knees for a bit.

Not half it won't. When I get to the top of the stairs the Pendulum Swingers are pouring out of the ballroom like there has been a thunderstorm at the nudist camp picnic. I have not seen so many wet, naked bodies since I peeped through the cracks in the back of the ladies' changing rooms at Tooting Bec baths. I look into the ballroom and the scene resembles a tropical rain forest by night—not that I have ever seen one, but I reckon it must be something like that. One or two couples who are probably stoned are still grinding away in the middle of the floor and one naked joker is lying on his back with his arms outstretched, chanting, "Now grow, you bastard!" as he gazes down at his acorn. Happy days!

Luckily there is no sign of Sam and Rosie and I am glad of this when I find Sid standing at my elbow sending glances into the darkness like cavalry scouts.

"Has she come yet?" says Sid nervously. "I wish I could get my hands on the bleeding basket who did this lot."

"Probably one of the residents," I say. "Oh—" My exclamation is caused by the sight of Rosie coming through the front door. She is bedraggled but fully clothed and alone. She must have got out by one of the side exits.

"Hello Sid, darling," she says, giving him a big hug, "what happened?"

"Some bleeder turned on the sprinkler system. Where have you been?"

"I've been struggling back from the theatre, love. My

cheap-jack brother couldn't afford a taxi. I might as well have stood under that lot, mightn't I?" She indicates the inside of the ballroom as the sprinklers are suddenly turned off. "Come on, Sid. Come and warm me up." She gives his arm a big squeeze and folds back her lips.

"I ought to—Oh, well. We'll do something about it in the morning." Sid shakes his head and is led away towards the stairs.

I go out of the front entrance of the hotel and look towards the pier. The moon is now high in the sky and there are a lot of stars about. Not a trace of rain. Luckily, in Rosie's capable hands, Sid is unlikely to ever know this.

CHAPTER EIGHT

"Old what?!" says Sid.

"Old Rottingfestians," I say.

"Who the hell are they?"

"They're a rugby club. Playing a couple of pre-season games in the area. Two teams and a spattering of wives, girlfriends and supporters. It can't be bad can it?"

"It can't be much worse."

It is two weeks after the Pendulum Society have wrung out their Y-fronts and gone home and the Cromby is now totally isolated from its adjoining buildings. On one side is a flat expanse of red mud with a few bricks sticking out of it and on the other the Irish problem are filling the air with dust and cursing. Bookings have dropped off at an alarming rate and some couples have only entered the hotel in order to ask for their deposits back. Never the most elegant of heaps, the Cromby now looks like the foreman's hut on a building site.

"At least they won't complain about the noise, I suppose," sighs Sid. This has been one of our main problems and "The Friends of Silence" checked out before breakfast on the first morning. Even Miss Primstone has taken to wearing ear plugs.

Poor Sid's enthusiasm has been fading fast and I know that only his pride is preventing him from selling out to Rigby. That little rat-substitute is frequently seen standing by his Rolls-Royce and supervising the demolition with an evil smile puckering the corners of his cake-hole.

Mum—Batwoman, as we now call her—and dad have long since returned to The Smoke and Rosie—thank God—has expressed herself as unwilling to risk Jason's tender lugholes until the noise of demolition has ceased.

"The little perisher hardly sleeps at the best of times," she says. "I'll come back when everything has settled down."

At this rate everything is going to settle like a ship sliding down in fifty fathoms of briny.

Elsewhere in the hotel things do not change much. Miss Ruperts spends most of her time in her room getting, or rather keeping, pissed, and Mrs. Caitley is now conducting a bitter vendetta with Senor Luigi, the latest head waiter. June, Audrey and Carmen roam the corridors, hoping to find Sacha Distel without his running shoes, and Sidney and Sandra play their own intimate version of mixed singles once a week. They have no trouble making ends meet but Dennis has to fiddle twice as hard in order to keep himself in fag money.

It is with the hotel in this, not untypically, fair-to-muddling situation that two important visitors arrive independently. The Old Rottingfestians Rugby Union Football Club, and Doctor Walter Carboy.

The former straggle up one Friday afternoon in a variety of fly-spattered M.G.s and scruffy 1100s. Those emerging from sports cars wear loud check hacking jackets and are usually accompanied by small blondes with brooches on the front of their jumpers. The 1100s disgorge a slightly older and shabbier article with leather elbow patches on their crumpled houndstooth and unlit pipes sagging over double chins. Their women have an air of experienced resignation like cows approaching the milking shed. You feel that they have been on tour before.

One feature that characterises all the men is an air of

undefeated cheerfulness that flows like something out of a Battle of Britain epic.

"How's it going, Tinker?"

"Dickers, old chap. Fantastic. How's Daphers?"

"Not so bad. Turned a bit green when I did a ton in Lewes High Street."

"Cool bastard! How did the peelers react to that?"

"No likey. I told them my grandmother was on the point of snuffing it but they wouldn't believe me. Good God! Look who's here. Tortor. What a marvellous surprise!" The bird smiles slowly and extends a cheek in order to protect her mouth. Tinker and Dickers descend on it hungrily and make sure that their hands do not feel left out of things. They grope clumsily as if there is more pleasure in being seen to grope rather than the actual groping.

One of the wives—this one must be a wife—looks very cute in her long sleeveless leather jacket, and I catch her eye as she turns away wearily from the hearty reunions going on around her. She raises a finger and I move to her side.

"Have you got a programme of what's on in the town?" she says.

"Yes, I expect so. It's probably a bit out of date, though. You'd be better off with the local paper. I'll see if I can find you one."

"That's very kind of you." She has a nice smile. "If you find one can you stick it in my pigeon hole? Number forty-two." A quick glance at her tidy little body and full lips confirms the coarse thought that I would not be at all averse to sticking it in her pigeon hole.

"Yes, of course," I say. "Going to make a real weekend of it, are you?"

"What do you mean?"

"I mean you'll be taking in some of the local entertainment as well as the rugby will you?"

"What do you mean 'as well as'?" she says. "Have you ever seen this lot on tour before? Unless you can drink your own weight in beer every evening you might as well buy a season ticket to the local chamber concerts, if you're ucky enough to find any. I don't expect to see Adrian again until Tuesday morning."

I begin to see what she means when by six o'clock they have drunk Dennis out of beer. It is the only thing they are interested in. As if there is some prize being offered they stand shoulder to shoulder pouring the stuff down their throats and threatening each other with physical violence in order to pay for the next round. With Dennis rushing around trying to find some more beer, they switch to shorts and so by supper time are in a decidedly jovial mood. It must be the first time in the history of the Cromby that forty-two male guests have marched into the dining room whistling "Colonel Bogey".

Some of the ladies, including my friend in forty-two, obviously find it less than amusing, but their menfolk sit down joyfully and immediately start pelting each other with bridge rolls and unscrew the top of the pepper pot so that their mates will pour the whole lot into their soup. Some joker has brought a farting cushion and this provides an endless source of amusement, especially when Sid comes out to try and restore some order. Every word he says is greeted by a loud raspberry. Senor Luigi tries to make headway with the bowing and scraping but when everybody jumps out of his chair and rests his chin on his chest every time he says anything, he eventually realises that they are taking the piss.

Only Mrs. Caitley knows how to handle the bastards. She storms out of the kitchen and tells them that she will stop serving any more food if they don't belt up. They give her a loud cheer, take a good butchers at the expression on her mush, and belt up.

After supper it is back to the bar and when I go to bed most of them are still at it. One or two of the younger birds stay with them but most of the wives watch tele, read a book or knit. I go into the tele lounge and ask if they would like anything.

"Yes, a husband," says one of them and the others laugh. "Don't hang around here too long," says another cute

133

little number who deserves better things, i.e. me. "Frustra tion might get the better of us."

I leave them, thinking that the wrong type of bloke coul easily be tempted to do himself a bit of good in the circum stances and retire to my room. By chance, Carmen drop by to see if I have any brown boot polish and in the ensuin search for a tin all thoughts of other ladies in the hotel ar driven rhythmically from my mind.

The next morning I wake up to find that one of the room has been burned out, due to a drunken Rottingfestrian fall ing asleep with a burning cigarette in his mitt. Numerou jokers have thrown up all over the hotel, and a runnin battle with fire buckets and soda syphons has kept most o the non-rugby-playing guests awake half the night. Ther is an angry queue forming outside Sidney's office and thei pointed chatter is loud enough to be heard above the nois of the Rottingfestrians pouring cornflakes over each othe in the dining room.

It is while explaining to the narked guests that Sidne will be along in a minute that I notice one of the birds wh was in the T.V. lounge, coming down to breakfast. She is bit older than the others and wearing a green silk trouse suit that does not have enough spare room in it to store postage stamp. She looks a very cool lady and sweeps he eyes over me like they are the lashes on a pair of wind screen wipers brushing aside an insect. Five minutes late Sidney comes along and the rugby hearties start pourin out of breakfast.

"O.K. chaps," trills one of them, "time for training. Thank God, I think, now for a little peace. But not a bit o it! They march straight across to the bar and demand pint all round. Dennis does not come on duty 'til eleven o'cloc and I try to point out this fact.

"Come off it!" snarls one of them, bigger and uglier tha the rest. "This is a hotel, isn't it? The bar should be ope all the time."

"I'd have thought you would have had enough la: night," I say. Fatso does not like this.

"It's not your place to comment on my drinking habits,

he yelps. "You do as you're told and get this bar open. Otherwise I'll report you to the B.T.A."

"You can report me to the R.S.P.C.A. if you like but the bar doesn't open 'til eleven."

"Damned cheek."

"Piss off."

"Grab him!"

Before I can lift a finger, or, more relevant to the situation, a boot, I am seized by half a dozen pairs of strong hands and pressed back against the wall.

"What shall we do with him?"

"Chuck him in the briny."

"No, I've got a better idea."

Five minutes later Sidney comes into the bar in answer to my shouts and looks around him inquiringly.

"I'm up here, Sid."

"Blimey!!" Sid has probably never seen me sitting astride a bison's head fifteen feet from the ground, and the hint of surprise in his voice is understandable.

"How long have you been up there?"

"Ever since they put me up here. Sid, you're going to have to get rid of them, you know."

"I can't afford to, Timmo."

"And Sid."

"Yes, Timmo."

"Get us a ladder before you piss off."

"Oh, sorry. O.K. Yeah. I'll do that." Sid seems to be in a daze as he wanders out of the room. My own feeling is of a deeper and more primitive nature. I am going to get even with those bastards if it is the last thing I do. You probably remember the movie. I was staked out on an anthill at the time and Yukon Pete and that sidewinding sidekick of his, the Mexican with the easy smile and the fast knife in the back pocket, had just lifted my stake in the Eldorado Gold Mine. That, after I had dug them both out of a roof-fall with my bare hands. Little did they know that three days later when I had gnawed through the buffalo hide thongs— "Ahem," the bird in the green trouser suit has succeeded in attracting my attention. "What were you thinking about?"

135

"Nothing," I gulp. "I was just thinking."

"It makes a refreshing change, even if it was about noth ing. What are you doing this afternoon?"

"I'm serving afternoon teas."

"I'd like you to serve me as well." The lady has no batted an eyelid—not that I would probably be able to tel if she had. I mean, do you know how to bat an eyelid?

"Come again?" I mumble.

"I hope so," she says briskly. "Come to my room at three Two-four-six."

"Aren't you going to the game?"

"This is the game, darling."

"I mean the rugger match."

"Darling, we all go on tour for different reasons. For some people it's rugby. Now me; I don't like team games. don't like mildewed jock straps, butterscotch socks, stuc mud in the bathroom basin, vomit on the door mat or cour gettes that talk like cucumbers. Do you understand me?"

"No."

"Two-four-six at three. We can discuss it further." She starts to willow away down the corridor as Fatso staggers ir through the door with his arms full of one-gallon beer cans

"Where the hell did you put the car keys?" he calls ou to her. "I've had to walk half a mile with this lot."

"I expect it did you the world of good, darling," she beams. "Why don't you try hopping upstairs on alternate feet. I'll time you."

"Bitch."

"Thank you." She draws herself up and makes with the withering glance. "Have a good game this afternoon, anc don't forget to put your jock strap on the right way round I'd hate your brain to get cold." She stalks off while I take in the glorious news that this must be Fatso's old lady Wild horses are going to be required to drag me away from room two-four-six.

Around lunch time the booze intake begins to drop a little and it becomes easier to spot those who are actually playing that afternoon. They can be seen sipping brandie rather than pints and ordering salads instead of meat anc

136

fourteen veg. Quite what difference this late change of diet is supposed to make I don't know. It must all be in the mind or whatever these blokes have instead. Half a dozen of them start rugby-passing empty beer cans round the foyer and Sandra gets a nasty belt in the bristols before they can be persuaded to stop.

It is while I am suggesting to Fatso and his friends that mouth to mouth resuscitation is not necessary that Doctor Carboy arrives. He is small, dapper, toothbrush-moustached and sports an unlit cigarette in a long gold cigarette holder.

"Step aside gentlemen," he says, putting a bulging attaché case on the reception counter. "I am a professional man. What seems to be the trouble, my dear?"

Sandra tells him in no uncertain fashion and Dr. C. shakes his head sadly. "Infectious high spirits cause serious complaints. Tell me, does this hurt?"

"Hey, wait a minute!"

"It's alright, my dear. I'm a doctor. Doctor Walter Carboy. No, I don't think there is anything there to worry about. Quite a lot to disturb, but nothing to worry about. In your case I'll waive my fee." He waves his hand towards the door. "Goodbye fee. Now, let's talk turkey—or Turkish —I don't mind. I would like the best room you have available and a bottle of Glen Grant sent up immediately. It doesn't matter about glasses, just send up the bottle. I joke, of course, madam," he smiles into Miss Primstone's bemused face. "And if you can do anything to turn off the noise next door and buy yourself a hairnet, I would be grateful. I need peace. Perfect peace."

"What about the rest of your luggage, sir?"

"It's following me from Southampton. Some of the most faithful luggage in the world. I've been trying to shake it off for years. And now gentlemen, enough of this idle badinage. Good luck with the spheroid and even better luck with the haemorrhoids, as my old coach used to say. Last one to my room is a cissy." And so saying he leaps towards the stairs like Rudolph Nureyev.

The Rottingfestrians are left speechless and it takes a few seconds before Miss Primstone shoves the keys of the Plaza

Suite into Martin's hands and tells him to catch up with Carboy fast.

"One of the old school," she says. "We have not seen his like for a long time." She is right there.

About two o'clock the hotel surrenders itself to blissful quiet as the Rottingfestrians pull out for their rugby match. They are full of booze and big talk about how they are going to crush the "swede-bashers" as they call the local side. Most of the wives and sweethearts troop along dutifully but there is no sign of green-pants, and the winsome chick who asked me about local events trips down the stairs ten minutes after the others have pulled out.

"Hurry up or you'll miss the match," I tell her.

"I'm not going. I thought I told you. I can't stand the game. I'm taking a look at the lifeboat station and the fish market. You don't fancy being my guide, do you?"

"I'd love to," I say, meaning it, "but I'm on duty this afternoon. Maybe tomorrow?"

"Maybe." She gives me a cute little wave and dances away down the steps. I think she quite fancies me, that one. It is diabolical isn't it? They are either all over you or nowhere to be seen.

Somehow the minutes tick by to three o'clock and my mind is not on the outcome of the clash between Hoverton R.U.F.C. and O.R.s.

Doctor Carboy rings down and asks if his baggage has arrived. We tell him "no" and he delivers half a dozen wisecracks and a request for a tailor, a shirtmaker and another bottle of Glen Grant to be sent up to his room. This is unheard of and Sid practically purrs with delight when we tell him.

"It's happening," he squeaks. "At last it's happening. Just when I had almost given up hope. I said if we stuck it out long enough the class customers would start showing up."

"No you didn't, Sid. Only this morning you were saying we should sell out to—"

"Quiet, you viper," hisses Sid. "Don't talk about things you don't understand."

138

"But I do understand, Sid. You seem to think that one swallower makes a summer."

"Belt up with those awful jokes and get the booze in. He's paying for it isn't he?"

"I hope so, Sid."

Ten minutes later simple Sid has disappeared, rubbing his hands together at the thought of the riches to come, and I am rubbing my hands nervously outside room number two-four-six, also thinking hopefully of the riches to come. I stretch out my arm but the door opens before I make contact with it.

"Come in."

"Blimey!"

Mrs. Fatso is wearing a black nylon negligee which is downright negligent in its coverage of her erogenous zones (I got the word from one of the sex books I borrowed from Battersea Public Library. "Everything you always wanted to know about sex but got smacked in the kisser for asking." Something like that, anyway).

"Come in," she says, "it's draughty with the door open."

"It would be draughty in the Sahara Desert with that thing on."

"You like it, do you?"

"Fantastic."

"I found my husband polishing the studs of his rugger boots with it."

"I don't believe it. I don't know how he can bear to leave the room with you looking like that." It is no hardship chatting her up. I mean what I am saying.

"He finds it easy to leave any room that doesn't have a bar in it. In the last three years he has only taken me out once, and that was to a film show of the British Lions tour of New Zealand followed by two blue movies. Most of those present were more turned on by the rugby film."

"Incredible."

"Sometimes I wonder if it's me."

"What do you mean?"

"I think I must be ugly or something. I look at myself in

139

the mirror and ask myself why he prefers a rugby ball to me."

"You're not ugly, you're a very striking woman."

"Thank you. I appreciate that. You're not just being kind?"

"No, no. Compared to some of the birds I—" I stop myself just in time. "Compared to most of the visitors we get, you're a knockout. I can't understand your husband. Has he always been like that?"

"He's always been mad keen on rugby. He started going off me about the time I stopped ironing his bootlaces."

"Why did he marry you in the first place?"

"Because the captain of the first team was going out with me. Basil is very competitive. He said he liked looking at me when I bent down to pour the teas."

"Oh, he noticed you, then?"

"Yes, he said that when I leaned over my breasts looked like two rugby balls dropping over the bar of my dress."

"Very romantic."

"It was, by his standards."

"What did you see in him?"

"Oh, physical things, I suppose. He wasn't so fat then. Somehow I thought that all those healthy young men charging about were where I ought to be. About as clever as a moth hanging round a naked flame. Talking of naked, will you take your clothes off please?"

"Gladly."

"Thank you. Basil doesn't believe in sex before a game and he's too tired afterwards, and he plays on Saturday and Sunday and trains every night of the week, so you can see that our marriage isn't exactly a hymn to fornication." My friend gives a little shiver and squeezes my arm passionately. I can see that her problem is one I am well equipped to solve and continue to unbutton my shirt.

"We rushed straight from the church to the Middlesex Sevens final at Twickenham. Basil described the selection of our Wedding Day as the biggest bog-up of his life. It's not surprising I give the impression of being hard, is it?"

" 'Hard' isn't the word I would have used." I slip my

140

hand inside her negligee and give one of her breasts an affectionate feel. Her whole body stiffens and she kisses me passionately on the mouth.

"Relax," I say, when I come up for air, "you're buckling my lips. Let's do it again more gently." I kiss her softly and run my finger lightly over the soft swell of her tummy. Now down, and she shivers again as my fingers brush against her minge fringe. Somewhere, on some foreign field, Fatso is buckling down for a scrum. Panting, puffing, aching. Poor devil. My heart goes out to him. That is all I can spare at the moment.

"O-o-o-h, that's good," murmurs Mrs. F. "You make me feel like a woman."

"You are a woman," I assure her. "We don't have to organise a poll."

"Talking of poles—" her cotton-picking fingers are trying to lead in a winner from my jockey briefs and my trousers have taken up their natural position around my ankles.

"You don't know how good this makes me feel." I am very happy for her. It is heartening to see her changing from the cool lady who deloused me with her eyes in the vestibule. She presses her body close to mine and starts nibbling my ear while her impatient fingers tug down my Marks and Spencers lingerie.

"O-o-o-h."

"Hang on a moment." Super-optimist that I am I have worn a pair of slip-on canvas shoes without socks so that the undressing bit can be effected tastefully and gracefully. These I ease off with the minimum of effort and step nimbly out of my trews. I would be a wiz at the bare-foot grape-pressing lark.

The state of the parties is now, Lea naked, Mrs. Fatso naked except for aforementioned sexy negligee. Like a master craftsman unwrapping a rare porcelain vase, I coax the black lace from her shoulders shedding a few delicate kisses along the length of her collar bone. I am contemplating a nibble-fest but Mrs. F. has other ideas. She sinks towards the ground faster than a British space rocket and wriggles her naked legs like a frisky mare waiting for the "off"—or in her case, the "on".

Some men might pause to hum the opening bars of Rule Britannia or comment on the rising price of butter, but not Timothy Lea. For a second, pregnant with a thousand anxieties and a million promises, I am poised at the entrance to her pleasure dome. Then, joyfully, inside it.

Oh, what fun we have in that drab room with the leaden sky outside. I catch a glimpse of sky sometimes. At the end of an hour I feel like a glove puppet that has been turned inside out so many times that its stitching has started to work loose.

We must have dozed off, because the next thing I recall is the sound of footsteps coming down the corridor. I glance at my watch and it is still far too early for Fatso to be back. Nevertheless, I am worried. The very fact that I am conscious of the noise makes me feel that my guardian angel (?) is trying to tell me something. Mrs. F. reacts to me sitting up and it is just as well that she does. Suddenly, from right outside the door, we hear a gruff male voice.

"Two-four-six did you say? Here we are." There is a knock on the door that coincides with the door knob turning.

I have to hand it to Mrs. F. She is on her feet before you can say "drop 'em" and gets to the door just as it starts opening.

"Oh, I'm sorry madam. I've got your husband here. He had a bit of an accident playing rugby." The bloke has obviously caught a glimpse of Mrs. F. in the altogether. He may hold back but hubby isn't going to. Oh, my gawd!! I glance round the room desperately but there is only a chest of drawers with a cupboard built on top of it. Even the bed clears the ground by only a measly two inches. What a lousy way to build a hotel. Before I can chuck myself out of the window, Fatso blunders into the room and steps on me. He curses and continues on his way to the bed.

Strange behaviour you might think but you cannot see him. He is holding a large wad of cotton wool over one of his eyes and the other is closed in sympathy. He is crumpled, battered and bruised and the groaning noises he is making sound very genuine.

"Dirty bastard puts his fingers in my eye. Ur-r-rgh!" He feels for the bed and collapses onto it face downwards.

I don't wait to ask if I can make him a cup of Nescafé but grab my clothes and head for the door. Outside, a St. John's Ambulance man is standing dutifully with his hat in his hand. His face adopts what is best described as a surprised expression as I skip past him.

"I'm the team mascot," I say comfortingly before I hare down the corridor.

CHAPTER NINE

The rest of the Old Rottingfestrians limp in from six o'clock until four the next morning. They have lost 48–3 and their spirits are lower than "God Bless America" on the Chinese Hit Parade. Drunk and despondent they are even worse than sloshed and sociable and I watch warily as they indulge in what are known as "pre-dinner drinkees". At least there is no sign of Fatso, and his lady wife favours me with a warm smile as she comes down to supper.

"I think he's going to live," she says, giving the inside of my thigh a discreet squeeze that can only be seen by Miss Primstone and half the people in the dining room. "He told me they got hammered. I said 'Darling, I know just how you feel'."

"Ye-e-es," I say, looking around nervously. "Let me find you a table."

"Are you going to serve me?" They must be able to see me blushing from the other end of the room. Not without difficulty I get her seated with my little friend who was looking at the market. Her husband has still not come back to the hotel and by the end of the meal the two birds are shooting me the kind of glances that make me wonder what they have been saying to each other.

I decide not to ask them and am popping back to my

room when Miss Ruperts waylays me. She is swaying slightly and I take the opportunity offered by helping her back to her office to remove the three beer bottle tops that have become lodged in her crotcheted shawl.

"I do want to talk to young Mr. Sidney," she says huffily. "He has been very naughty lately. I am convinced he is trying to avoid me." She is dead right there. Sid is at last coming round to my way of thinking and after the Pendulum Society and the Old Rottingfestrians is a lot less keen on the convention idea. "I have a very interesting proposition to discuss with him," she goes on. "I am convinced it could be of great benefit to us all."

"I'm certain it could be," I say, humouring her. "When I see Mr. Noggett I'll tell him to come and see you."

"Please do. You see I have an uncle, by one of those quirks of fate not greatly older than myself, and he—"

"Yes, yes," I say, "well, I must be going." I am backing out just as Doctor Carboy bowls in.

"Dear lady," he trills, "What can I say." He looks round the dark, shabby room like it is an Ideal Home feature. "Your own incomparable beauty is matched by the elegance of your surroundings. Forgive me for not coming sooner but I was engaged in a tedious search for my baggage. Alas, without success. But what care I. You are the prettiest little baggage in the world." I think he must be round the twist but Miss Ruperts giggles coyly and obviously laps it up. No accounting for tastes.

"Go and make sure that the champagne is cool," he says to me. "I'll make sure that the blood is hot." He is actually taking her hand in his as I leave. I always thought he was a bit batty, now I am certain of it.

"I reckon your Miss Ruperts is on the point of betraying you with another," I say, when I bump into Sidney. "That Doctor Carboy bloke is giving her the full treatment."

"If only we had a few more like him, all our troubles would be over," sighs Sidney. "I hope she doesn't upset him. You know, I think you were right about her. I can't afford the booze she puts away, let alone anything else.

Trouble is I suppose Mrs. Caitley would chuck in her notice if I gave her the boot."

"Mrs. Caitley would probably punch your head in, Sid. Come on, why fight it any longer? This place is going down the drain. If there's anything left when these bleeding rugger buggers have pulled out, why don't you let Rigby have it?"

Sid sighs and does the whole head-shaking bit, like Jack Hawkins about to send Richard Todd out on a suicide mission without his cocker spaniel. "Oh, blimey," he says, "after all I've put into the place." I can't think of anything, but maybe he is talking about a different place. "All right," he goes on, "but the bastard will have to come to me first. I'm not crawling back to him."

Sidney does not have to wait long for the coming. The next morning, while I am helping June and Audrey clean up the results of a fire extinguisher battle—no prizes for guessing who between—Rigby's rodent frame bristles behind us.

"You want to try using carpet shampoo," he says. "It's less messy. Where's Noggett? Hiding from his creditors, as usual?"

"I suggest you wait in the lounge," I say grandly. "I'll tell him you're here."

"No thanks. Something might drop off the walls."

"I thought that's how you got in here," says June, loyally.

"Watch it, girlie, you'll find yourself out of a job when I take over," snarls Rigby.

"I wouldn't stay here five minutes if you took over. Only long enough to open the windows."

You don't have to be good at reading expressions to know that Rigby does not like that, but before he can say anything Sidney appears.

"You're looking for me, are you?" he says, seeing Rigby.

"Amongst many others, I expect," sneers Rigby. "I came round to tell you that I'm fed up with hanging about. Unless you see sense by tomorrow dinner-time I'm moving my boys in to start developing the sites on either side of you. They'll be at it twenty-four hours a day, working by flood-lights. I'm behind schedule and my backers want results.

If you don't take my offer you won't be able to accept a booking from anyone who isn't deaf."

"You can't blackmail me."

"I'm not blackmailing you. I'm telling you. You should be grateful to me for giving you a chance to get out of this dump. Look at it! I'm amazed it hasn't fallen down without the other two buildings to support it."

"You're a nice bloke to do business with, aren't you?" Sid's fists have folded into bunches of bananas and there is a look in his eye like the outbreak of World War III.

"I've heard about the kind of guests you're taking now. Down to football teams, isn't it? I suppose if they can't afford the Y.M.C.A. they come here."

"Rugby teams, not football teams." The words come from one of Fatso's mates and are spoken without warmth. Since the speaker is about six foot eight inches tall they encourage attention.

"Rugby teams," says Rat Features.

"And we never stay at the Y.M.C.A. The Y.W.C.A., now that's different." Mr. Big is advancing towards Rigby as if he wants to use him to practise tying knots.

"Of course."

"Piss off," says Sid, falling in beside the incredible hulk.

"Dinner time tomorrow," squeaks Rigby, breaking the World Backward-walking record. "If you don't agree to my terms, I'll turn my boys loose on the site."

"Getoutofit!!!"'

Rigby flashes into his Rolls like he is only let out of it on a spring. The windows are a smokey-blue colour so we cannot see him through them. Nobody expresses a sense of loss.

"We'll see him tomorrow," says the big guy. There is a note of anticipation in his voice that I do not appreciate at the time.

"What are we going to do, Sid?" I say.

"I don't know, Timmy. It just depends on what kind of offer he finally makes." But, from the expression on Sid's face I know that he has as good as chucked in the sponge.

One person who remains cheerful is Miss Ruperts. When

146

I next see her, she squeezes my arm affectionately and draws me closer. She opens her mouth to speak and I feel that it must conceal the entrance to a whisky still.

"He's so kind and thoughtful, isn't he?" she says.

"Who?"

"Doctor Carboy. Or Walter as he allows me to call him. Do you know he's going to have all my jewellery valued free?"

I look at her mitts and they are indeed ringless.

"Very nice." It is isn't it? Doctor Carboy has now completely replenished the items that were lost when his luggage failed to turn up and the local tradespeople must be very grateful for his custom. He has also consumed gallons of booze and exotic goodies in the privacy of his suite. All in all, a man well versed in the art of chucking money about. Now he has taken Miss Ruperts' jewellery—hey! Wait a minute. I detach myself from Miss Ruperts and move swiftly to Sid's side. He is in his office slamming shut a large ledger and beginning to slide despairing hands over his mush.

"Sid," I say, trying to sound very relaxed about the whole thing, "has it occurred to you that Doctor Carboy might be a conman?" Sid pauses for a moment, then continues to slide despairing hands over his mush.

"Not until you mentioned it," he says. "Now it seems the most natural thing in the world. That's all we need, isn't it? A conman. Very nice. When did you first become suspicious?"

I tell Sid about the ring-valuing and he shakes his head.

"He just might be on the level," he says hopefully. "Come on, we'd better go and talk to Miss Ruperts. I've been trying to keep out of her way but I suppose—"

"You've been avoiding me," says Miss Ruperts reproachfully when we interrupt her trying to find room for a couple of ice cubes in a jumbo slug of scotch.

"I've been very busy," says Sid, lamely. "Now—"

"Now," says Miss Ruperts, riding over him professionally. "Now that you're here at last. There's something I want to say to you—"

"Yes, but—"

147

"Doctor Carboy."

"Oh." Sid's cake-hole closes slowly.

"A wonderful man and a wonderful doctor. He has performed miracles for me in the short time he has been here. Not one of your killjoys," she raises her glass to the absent Doctor C. and knocks back a Bogart-sized swig. Sid winces. "Now, what I have been vainly trying to tell you for the last few days is that I have inherited an extraordinarily large sum of money," she pauses while Sid and I gulp. "Some relation I hardly knew I had. Made a fortune in rubber. Quite remarkable what he did with it. The rubber I mean." Sid nods understandingly. "Now, I am very happy here, and so is my friend Mrs. Caitley, but neither of us is getting any younger," she takes another giant swig, "and what I was thinking is that it might well be a good idea to turn the hotel into a clinic under the supervision of Doctor Carboy. In that way the interests of many of the more elderly members of the staff could be preserved and you would still have a profitable investment. Possibly a much more profitable investment."

"And you would be prepared to put some of your money into the venture, would you, Miss Ruperts?" Sid's tone could be described as pleading.

"With Doctor Carboy at the helm I would have no qualms about putting my money into anything."

"It sounds a marvellous idea, Miss Ruperts. I have considered something like it myself. But are you certain that Doctor Carboy is the right man? Does he really have the—"

"Without Doctor Carboy I would not consider putting up a penny." Miss Ruperts bangs down her empty glass on the table and the ice cubes land in it a couple of seconds later.

"Well, it's certainly a very interesting idea, isn't it, Timmy?"

"Very interesting, Sid."

"We'd better go and have a word about it, hadn't we, Timmy?"

"Yes, Sid."

148

"Have you—er, mentioned your idea to Doctor Carboy yet, Miss Ruperts?"

"No. I thought it right that I should speak with you first."

"Very thoughtful of you. Does he—er, know about your good fortune?"

"The inheritance? No. I didn't want to appear ostentatious."

"Very sensible," says Sid, having no idea what she is on about. "Well, we'll come back to you very soon."

When we get to Carboy's room it is empty—and I mean empty. Even the toothmugs have gone and there is no trace of all the booze we have carted up there.

"Oh my gawd." Sid sinks down on the bed, a beaten man.

"Hey, Sid, look!" A freshly stubbed fag end is still smoking in one of the ash trays. "He must have only just left."

Sid beats me to the door leading to the back stairs by a short head and it is a good race to lose. He storms through and promptly dives over a bulky suitcase waiting on the top step. At the same instant an empty-handed Carboy appears, presumably coming back to collect his last load of swag. He is a cool bastard because he carefully steps over the suitcase and extends a helping hand to Sid.

"My goodness me. You nearly took a nasty tumble, didn't you? Very unpleasant." He indicates the suitcase. "I rather think that this case contains some of the items that were stolen from my room."

"Really," says Sid.

"Yes, I returned a few minutes ago to find it ransacked. You really will have to tighten up on your security precautions."

"We have it very much in mind," says Sid, wincing as he tries to lift the suitcase. "Blimey, the bloke certainly stashed some stuff away, didn't he?"

"Indeed, indeed. But I suspect that there is even more somewhere. I think I'll take another look round the yard to see if I can spot what he's done with it."

"We'll come with you," says Sid quickly. "Mr. Lea is our house detective, you know."

"Really. You want to keep on your toes young man. Wouldn't it be better if you—er, rang the police?"

"We'll do that later."

Directly outside the back entrance is a Cortina Estate with the boot packed roof-high with suitcases.

"I think we might just have found where the rest of the stuff is," says Sid drily.

"All that? It never occurred to me—"

"Doctor Carboy, or whatever your name is, you're not fooling anybody. We know you lifted that stuff."

"What?" Carboy's display of indignant outrage is worth a government subsidy. "How dare you! Do you know what you're suggesting?"

"I'm suggesting we have a little chat," says Sid. "Believe it or not I've got a proposition to make to you."

It is about two o'clock in the morning when I go to bed and Carboy is still maintaining that somebody else nicked all the stuff from the rooms. Yes, it turns out that about half a dozen rooms have been turned over. He is, not surprisingly, very interested in Miss Ruperts' proposition and when I leave Sid and him they are on the point of going off to see the old bag. One thing that does cheer and amaze me is that Carboy really is a doctor. At least he says he is and he has a very impressive piece of paper to back his words. It carries more swirls and squiggles than the label on a vermouth bottle.

The next morning I come down to find that Carboy and Miss Ruperts have left for London.

"That's it," I tell Sid. "He's probably married her by now. We'll be right in the S — H one T."

"Whether he has or hasn't he can't do us too much harm. I still own this hotel and if he gets nasty I'll tell Miss Ruperts what he was up to last night. He'll find it difficult to talk his way out of that."

"Don't bet on it. He hasn't been doing badly so far. That geezer could dive into a cesspool and come up smelling like a pouf's bedroom. Why have they gone to London?"

"She wants him to get all the gen. on her financial affairs."

"Bleeding heck! He'll take her to the cleaners. Why didn't you go?"

"She didn't want me to. I don't have the same pull that he does. Let's face it. Any deal we fix up is because she reckons him."

Much as it pains me to admit it, I know that Sid is right and that there is nothing we can do except twiddle our thumbs and wait for Carboy and Ruperts to turn up again —if they ever do. Even as I think about it I have a horrible vision of them climbing the gang-plank of the Q.E. II, arm in arm . . .

Luckily there are other things to take my mind off my immediate problems. Things like Mrs. Fatso. She willows up to me, removing a crumb from the corner of her beautiful mouth and fixing me with an eye that glows like a night-watchman's brazier.

"There's another game this afternoon," she says pointedly.

"Your old man going to be up to it?"

"Wild horses wouldn't drag him away."

"And you're not going?"

"He might get hurt again. I couldn't bear to watch that." She smoothes a non-existent ruckle out of her slacks. Slacks! There's a ridiculous word for them. There is more tension going on down there than at a meeting of the Labour Party Executive. "I was thinking that it might be fun to organise a little team activity of our own. Quite a number of the girls aren't all that keen on rugger."

Hello, hello! What's all this then? Do I detect intimations of immorality? (It's wonderful what a course at the Polytechnic can do for your vocabulary, isn't it?)

"Oh, yes," I say, dead casual. "I saw you talking to one of your friends."

"Judy? Yes, she was very keen on the idea. She feels the fish market has little more to offer her."

"Very understandable. Quite what was she considering as an alternative?"

"Well," Mrs. Fatso takes a deep breath. Something she does rather well. "A party might be fun, mightn't it? If you could round up some more able-bodied men we might pass the afternoon in more agreeable fashion than standing on a sodden touch-line shouting 'olly, olly, Rotting-festrians'."

"Sounds a very nice idea. My colleague, Mr. Noggett, has a suite of rooms which would be ideal for the purpose. I'm certain he would be only too glad to participate."

"Can't you think about anything else but nooky at a time like this?" says Sid irritably when I tell him.

"No. What is there?" Sid thinks for a moment.

"You're right. What time does the party start?"

I tell him that I have laid it on for when all the Rotting-festrians have trotted off to the rugby game and his face creases into a faint smile for the first time in days.

"Frisky load of fillies, aren't they?" he says. "I won't be sorry to get amongst that lot after what I've been through with their old men. Now we've only got to worry about stalling Rigby."

To my surprise, Rigby does not show up promptly at lunch time and it is only when the Rottingfestrians are having their last pint before leaving for the game that the Rolls slides up outside the hotel entrance. Its arrival draws a cheer from the crowd of half-pissed thicknecks milling about outside the bar and this does not go down well with Rigby.

"Take a good look," he sneers, indicating the car. "It's about as near as any of you will ever get to one."

This remark provokes an immediate outcry and Sid moves forward fast to avoid a possible lynching.

"Come and have a drink," he says civilly. Rigby jerks his head towards the bar.

"Not in here, thanks. I don't like drinking with scruffy schoolkids."

"Come into the office." Sid leads the way to Miss Ruperts' cubby hole and we are fortunate enough to find half a bottle of scotch that the old bat has left over from breakfast.

"I'm not here to pay a social call. Are you ready to sign?"

"We've given it a lot of thought—"

"You've had a lot of time."

"—but we won't be able to give you our decision until tomorrow."

"Right! Well, you're going to have a sleepless night to think about it. I'm walking straight out of here and I'm giving my boys the go ahead to start moving in. You'd better start getting the cotton wool out of the medicine cabinet."

"Mr. Rigby? How fortunate to find you here." The words fall from the lips of Doctor Carboy who comes bustling through the door carrying a bulging briefcase. Hard behind him is Miss Ruperts, her face flushed with what I imagine to be a few hastily snatched glasses of lunch.

"Who is this?" snarls Rigby.

"I represent those interests of this lady and gentleman that are not covered by liquor, sex and drugs," says Carboy evenly. "I have been bringing myself up to date with their affairs. I had to go to London to read all the relevant Sunday newspapers."

"I'm not interested in jokes," says Rigby, sourly.

"What a pity. With a face like that I'd have thought you would have had to have been."

"I didn't come here to be insulted."

"No, I'm certain a man of your standing can be insulted anywhere. In fact, now I come to mention it, I'm certain a man of your standing could be standing anywhere. Like outside in the rain for instance. There's a Rolls-Royce outside the front door. Why don't you go and stand under it and I'll tell you when it's stopped raining."

"Do you know who I am?" screeches Rigby.

"Of course I do. You're King Farouk's younger brother thinking that nobody is going to recognise you without the flower pot and the dark glasses. Don't be ridiculous. Of course I know who you are. I told you when I came in. Don't say you've forgotten already?"

"Don't beat about the bush, Walter," pants Miss Ruperts,

casting about her for the whisky bottle. "Tell him. Odious little man."

"I beg your pardon."

"Not you, Walter! Him!"

"Very well. If you insist, dear lady. I'm sorry, Ratby, I mean Rigby, but I'm afraid you've been taken over."

"What!" Rigby's face turns a different shade of scarlet.

"Yes. The Rigram Property Company is now owned by a consortium in which my fair companion here is the major shareholder. Yes, Rigby, money talks, and to you it says: 'Shove off and see if you can get a job posing for a Warfarine advertisement.'"

"You expect me to believe that?"

"I don't care whether you believe it or not. Why don't you ring your accountant? Mr. Ransome, isn't it?" Rigby's face achieves another remarkable change of shade. "How did you—?"

"Suffice to say that we have ways, Rigby. Now if you will excuse me. I have to cut my toenails and I don't want anyone to get hurt by flying trimmings."

"I'll get—"

"'Out' is all you're entitled to get at the moment." There is a hard edge to Carboy's voice that suggests that he does not spend all his time helping old ladies across badly marked zebra crossings. Rigby looks round desperately.

"You haven't heard the last of this. I'll be in touch."

"I'll buy a pair of gloves just in case. Good afternoon." Carboy opens the door and Rigby storms out. The minute he has gone we both turn on Carboy.

"Is that true? Have you really taken over that bastard's outfit?"

"Virtually. Miss Ruperts has secured a controlling interest in it. To all intents and purposes she is the owner."

"And you did all that in a couple of hours?"

"I know the right people."

"I'll say you do."

"I think a glass of champagne would be in order," trills Miss Ruperts.

"I'll drink to that," says Carboy. "Now what on earth is all that noise about?"

We bundle out into the foyer and there is a tall geezer wearing a grey chauffeur's uniform and a very worried expression.

"What's the matter?"

"Bloody young hooligan has driven off in Mr. Rigby's Rolls."

"Where's Rigby?"

"He's inside it!"

"Blimey!"

We join the drunken crowd of Rottingfestrians laughing and cheering on the steps of the hotel and follow their eyes towards the pier.

"What's Lofty going to do with him?" Oh, so that's it. I thought the big fellow had got the needle with Rigby. Little did I know how much.

"Good God. He's driving onto the pier!!" He is too. For some reason they have opened the gates and I can see ant-like figures hopping out of the way as the black shape zooms behind the ghost train.

"He's going it, isn't he?"

"Slow down Lofty, you Charley!"

"Oh, no!!" The Rolls is now ripping down the pier like it is a runway.

"What's he doing?"

"He's pissed."

"He's mad."

"He won't be able to stop."

The last speaker is right. As we watch, horrified, the Rolls bursts through the barrier like it is made of bread sticks and dives gracefully into the sea.

"Oh, my God."

Some of the onlookers start running towards the pier but most of us remain rooted to the spot.

"Look!"

To my amazement a figure appears on the surface closely followed by another. There is a pause and then they both begin to swim slowly towards the pontoon at the end of the pier. A relieved cheer goes up.

"Did he have his kit with him?" says Fatso seriously.

"Come on, let's go and clap him in."

"Better hurry or we'll be late for the kick off."

"Time for another beer?"

"No. We'll have one there." They pick up boots and bags and disappear in a straggling convoy.

"Marvellous, isn't it?" says Sid.

"Fantastic," says Carboy. "Come my dear, the champagne awaits."

They go in and Sid rests his hand on my shoulder.

"Might as well have a glass of bubbly, I suppose."

"Yoo hoo."

We look up and there are Mrs. Fatso and Judy and two other well-stacked birds leaning over the balcony of Sid's room. They all appear to be wearing low-cut negligees and it looks like the production line of a small dumpling factory looming down on us.

"Did you tell Petheridge to fall in for this lot?" says Sid, rubbing his hands together.

"Yeah, I told him I'd wake him up when the party started."

"Don't bother. He's been working a bit hard lately and I think we can handle this lot by ourselves."

THE END

❧ GRAHAM MASTERTON ❧

MAIDEN VOYAGE

The year is 1924 – the year of dizzy flappers, champagne baths and wild parties in the purple dawn. It is also the year of the maiden voyage of a fabulous Transatlantic luxury liner, the SS *Arcadia* – and a first for sparkling Catriona Keys, transformed overnight from carefree partygoer to powerful head of giant Keys Shipping. Enter young Mark Beeney, handsome but dangerous American shipping magnate, who is about to launch a daring takeover bid for Keys Shipping – and for Catriona's heart. As the champagne bubbles above decks, Keys Shipping is about to sail into troubled waters . . .

MAIDEN VOYAGE is an enthralling saga of destiny and decadence, passion and power – a wonderful epic recreation of the glamour and excitement of a bygone age.

GENERAL FICTION   0 7221 6028 3   £2.50

LEONARD ROSSITER

THE LOWEST FORM OF WIT

Sarcasm is the lowest form of wit – no one is beneath using it – but it is also the most satisfying. There is no greater pleasure than pinning your squirming victim to the dinner-table with a carefully sharpened and coolly aimed insult or flooring him with a sudden and crippling kick beneath the belt.

Sarcasm requires deadly accuracy and perfect timing. It is the most skilful kind of unarmed combat and because no holds are barred it is also the most dangerous. THE LOWEST FORM OF WIT is a complete handbook for aspiring masters and mistresses of sarcasm compiled by Leonard Rossiter, a black belt of this vicious art. He tells you everything you need to know about sarcasm from its low-down role in history to specific advice on dealing with traffic wardens, bank managers, neighbours, foreigners and other despicable persons.

This is a treasury of biting jibes and stinging retorts which explores the lowest kind of wit in the highest kind of style.

HUMOUR   0 7221 7513 2   £1.50

The Book Of
ROYAL
LISTS

CRAIG BROWN & LESLEY CUNLIFFE

What should you serve the Royal Family if they drop in for dinner?
How does the Queen keep her Corgies content?
Which clergyman did Prince Charles throw into the fountain at Balmoral?
What are Princess Diana's favourite sweets?
Which television programmes does the Queen Mother like best?
How can you recognise a Royal racing pigeon?

The Royal Family is no ordinary family, and Royal Lists are not like ordinary lists. Here at last are the answers to all the questions that have intrigued dedicated Royal-watchers, loyal patriots, convinced monarchists and the millions of adoring fans around the world who follow every move of Britain's first family.

THE BOOK OF ROYAL LISTS is the most comprehensive collection of information ever assembled about the British Royal Family and their ancestors. Witty and informed, amusing but respectful, it surprises, charms and dazzles.

HUMOUR   0 7221 1934 8   £2.50

A SELECTION OF BESTSELLERS FROM SPHERE

FICTION

THE MISTS OF AVALON	Marion Bradley	£2.95 ☐
THE INNOCENT DARK	J. S. Forrester	£1.95 ☐
THURSTON HOUSE	Danielle Steel	£1.95 ☐
MAIDEN VOYAGE	Graham Masterton	£2.50 ☐
THE FURTHER ADVENTURES OF HUCKLEBERRY FINN	Greg Matthews	£2.95 ☐

FILM AND TV TIE-INS

THE IRISH R.M.	E. E. Somerville and Martin Ross	£1.95 ☐
SCARFACE	Paul Monette	£1.75 ☐
THE KILLING OF KAREN SILKWOOD	Richard Rashke	£1.95 ☐
THE RADISH DAY JUBILEE	Sheilah B. Bruce	£1.50 ☐
THEY CALL ME BOOBER FRAGGLE	Michaela Muntean	£1.50 ☐
RED AND THE PUMPKINS	Jocelyn Stevenson	£1.50 ☐

NON-FICTION

GRENADA: INVASION, REVOLUTION AND AFTERMATH	Hugh O'Shaughnessy	£2.95 ☐
DIETING MAKES YOU FAT	Geoffrey Cannon & Hetty Einzig	£1.95 ☐
THE FRUIT AND NUT BOOK	Helena Radecka	£6.95 ☐
LEBANON, THE FRACTURED COUNTRY	David Gilmour	£2.95 ☐
THE OFFICIAL MARTIAL ARTS HANDBOOK	David Mitchell	£3.95 ☐

All Sphere books are available at your local bookshop or newsagent, or can be ordered direct from the publisher. Just tick the titles you want and fill in the form below.

Name _____

Address _____

_____

Write to Sphere Books, Cash Sales Department, P.O. Box 11, Falmouth, Cornwall TR10 9EN

Please enclose a cheque or postal order to the value of the cover price plus:

UK: 45p for the first book, 20p for the second book and 14p for each additional book ordered to a maximum charge of £1.63.

OVERSEAS: 75p for the first book and 21p per copy for each additional book.

BFPO & EIRE: 45p for the first book, 20p for the second book plus 14p per copy for the next 7 books, thereafter 8p per book.

Sphere Books reserve the right to show new retail prices on covers which may differ from those previously advertised in the text or elsewhere, and to increase postal rates in accordance with the PO.